I0630111

A MODERN MIDLIFE CHRISTMAS CAROL

ALANA OXFORD

8N PUBLISHING

Cover design by Purpose on Paper

Editing by Heather Hollister

Proofreading by Chloe Massarello

ISBN: 979-8-9879774-9-1

eBook ISBN: 979-8-9879774-8-4

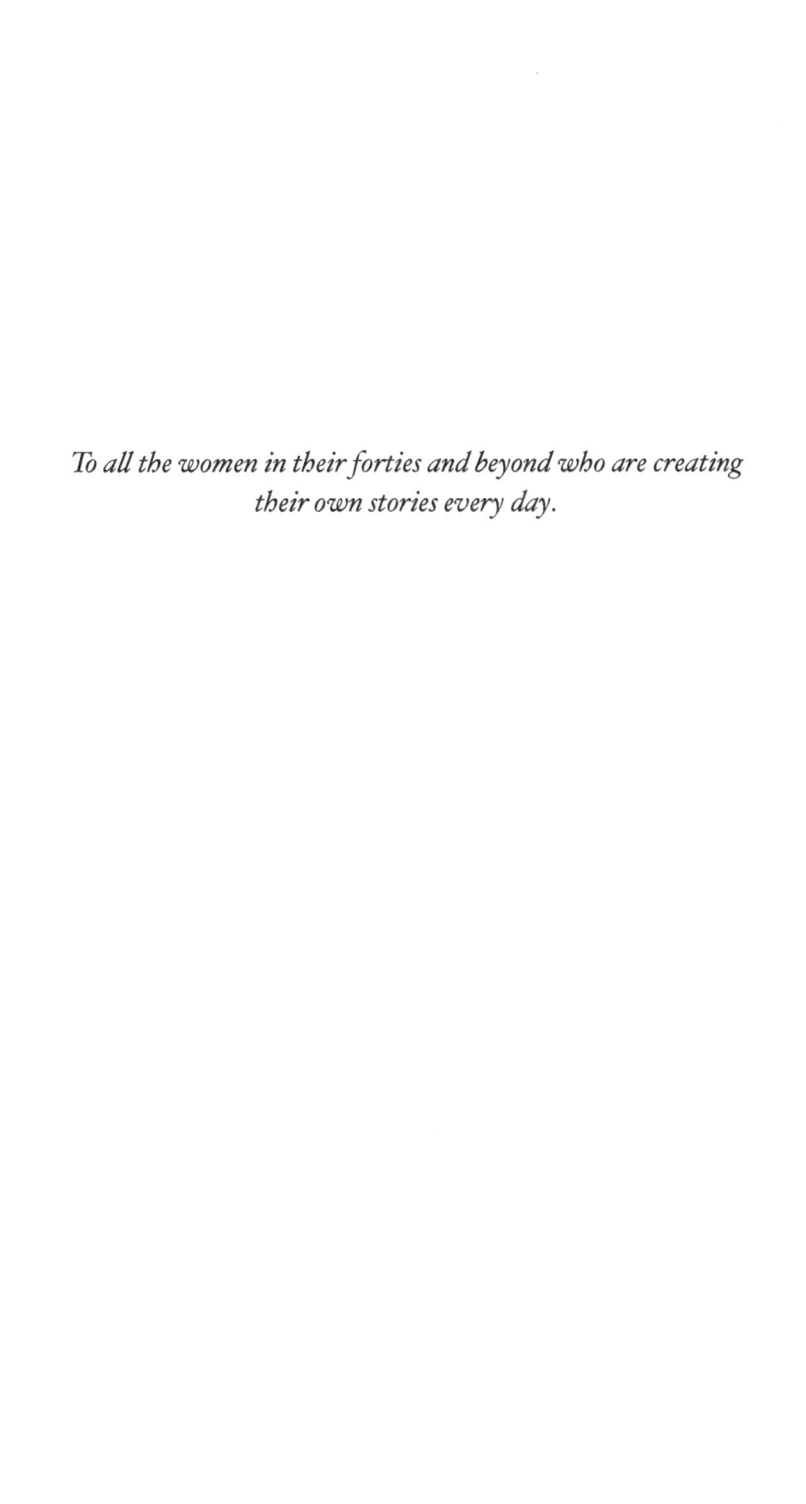

To all the women in their forties and beyond who are creating their own stories every day.

THE GHOST OF CHRISTMAS SPIRIT

Christmas cheer was dead, to begin with.

Its death knell tolled as Jacob walked into the bathroom. Scratch that. More like strutted into the bathroom with a goofy grin on his face.

Eliza was soaking in the tub, enjoying one of the few luxuries afforded to her in regular life. Her mother had called her three times that day, each time with a different problem she wanted Eliza to solve for her. First it was a crisis about her mother's lax snow removal service, then to lament the styling capabilities of the hairdresser she was never happy with but refused to stop going to, and finally to tell Eliza to accompany her to an eye appointment the following week. She was in her eighties, after all. She could pass at any moment so Eliza needed to get this taken care of ASAP. Naturally, the best time to do it was before Christmas when things were "winding down for the year." Besides, the medical scheduler made the appointment and her mother had to take it, otherwise nothing would get done for months and months.

That was more than enough for one day, but Eliza had also picked up her son and daughter from high school after her shift at the bookstore. In the car, she'd asked them to get dinner started so she could take a bath to shake off the stress of the day. The kids had grunted in a way that acknowledged their mother had spoken to them, but not necessarily that they agreed. They hadn't argued, so Eliza's busy brain ticked that off as something taken care of and moved on to the next item of business.

Everyone in the house knew that if Eliza was in the bath, she should be left alone for at least half an hour, unless there was a real emergency she needed to deal with. She'd only been in the water for ten minutes when Jacob burst in, startling her.

She sat up from her nest of steaming, lavender scented bubbles.

"What's wrong?" she asked, instantly going from tentative relaxation to minor panic.

"Nothing's wrong," Jacob beamed. "We've just been invited to Edward and Dymond's for the week of Christmas!"

Eliza's panic rose. Her mind's eye called up an image of her brother-in-law Edward's smug face. Equally unsettling was the heavily made up face of his very young second wife, Dymond. These were not people she wanted to contemplate while in the safe haven of her tub.

"Edward and Dymond? They never invite us over for

anything. Besides, we already have plans to make dinner at my mom's for Christmas."

Jacob knew the plan. Eliza couldn't wrap her head around the reason he would burst in and tell her such irrelevant things.

Jacob shook his head, big silly smile still on his face.

"We'll do dinner with her another time. I told Edward we'd be there."

The hot bath might as well be filled with ice cubes. There would be no relaxation now.

"What do you mean you said we'd be there? My mom's going to lose her shit if we change the plan now. It's only three weeks before Christmas!"

"She'll get over it," Jacob dismissed Eliza's protest. "We hardly ever see my brother. We always see your mom. It'll be a nice change of scenery for all of us. Plus, Dymond and Edward will be hosting so you can just sit back and relax. It'll be like a vacation."

The words "vacation" and "Edward and Dymond" did not go together in Eliza's mind. "Disaster" was more like it.

Surely, Jacob knew what an impossible change it would be to swap a twenty minute drive to her mom's house for a five hour drive from their Grand Rapids, Michigan home to Edward's Cincinnati, Ohio mansion. Not only was it ludicrous, but it was so much more work that she'd have to do. She was actually on top of Christmas preparations for a change. She couldn't face starting at zero now. There would be extra laundry and packing and the nightmare of gift purchasing to contend with. She was done with buying gifts. The closer to Christmas, the worse the shopping experience.

Eliza had no desire to enter into that frenzied madhouse known as shopping in December.

"You seriously want to go to Edward's?" Eliza was genuinely shocked. Jacob and his older brother weren't particularly close. Edward's main personality trait was being a pretentious jackass, whereas Jacob had more of a practical dreamer thing going on. Edward's favorite topics of conversation were his swelling bank account and the plethora of material possessions he was quickly amassing. It was tedious and, in Eliza's opinion, crass.

Jacob and Eliza were financially comfortable, but Eliza tended to have a more conservative approach to spending. They had the kids to consider, so it made sense that they think through big purchases and analyze their priorities together. They didn't always agree on what those priorities should be, but they had what they needed, most of what they wanted, and that was good enough for them. Even though they weren't lacking, Eliza found it grating to politely smile and nod along to Edward cataloging his own wealth, with that irritating pompous voice of his.

As if flaunting his wealth wasn't bad enough, Edward was wont to make things into a competition. If Jacob had gotten a new car for his family, then Edward was quick to mention the even newer and more expensive car he'd gotten for himself. If Jacob got a promotion at work, Edward had made a ridiculously lucrative invest-ment. If Jacob took the family on a summer road trip to northern Michigan, Edward had booked a Caribbean cruise, a three-week European tour, and a two-week anniversary trip to Monte-Carlo with Dymond.

Edward had been part of her family since she'd

married Jacob twenty years ago, but they weren't anywhere near close enough that she could call him out. Not that she would anyway. She'd been raised to be polite and gracious and giving anyone an earful of her negative feelings just wouldn't do. She wished Jacob would tell him off, but he was under some sort of spell of Edward's. Having no siblings herself, it wasn't a dynamic she had firsthand knowledge of. Although, she'd seen enough arguing between her own kids, Bella and Bobby, to doubt they'd ever let the other get away with anything. She hoped it meant she'd done something right by her kids, but the longer she was at this parenting thing, the less sway she felt her influence had on them.

Before she could wander down the path of "what ifs" that had become increasingly familiar since entering her forties, Jacob brought her back to the matter at hand.

"Of course I want to go to Edward's! He's got a great place. It'll be like staying at a resort for Christmas, only we don't have to pay for it! Plus, it'll do the kids good to spend some time with their cousin."

Eliza sighed. It may not be monetary but she was sure she'd pay dearly for this trip. So would the kids. The cousin in question was three-year-old Derby. His mother, Dymond, fit the role of stereotypical midlife crisis second wife. Whereas Edward's first wife, Michelle, was only two years younger than him, Dymond was twenty-six to Edward's fifty-four. They'd been married for three years, which was just after Edward and Michelle's divorce had gone through. He'd gotten Dymond pregnant before leaving Michelle and their three nearly grown children. They hadn't really seen those cousins since. It could have been a Jerry Springer episode.

Bella and Bobby were firmly in their sulky teenage years. They weren't going to be thrilled to spend their Christmas break entertaining a hyperactive and ill-behaved preschooler. They hadn't liked the prospect of quietly sitting around their elderly grandmother's house for one day. A whole week with Derby wasn't going to go over well.

She didn't see how Christmas would be a pleasant time to spend with them in their over-the-top mansion of a home. Eliza could only imagine what outrageous new things Edward and Dymond had purchased or done since the last time they'd see them. The Christmas gifts wouldn't be sincere either. They'd be a competition and she didn't want to spend her and Jacob's hard-earned money buying expensive junk for unappreciative people.

"I don't know if this is such a good idea..." Eliza struggled to find a way to convey that spending time with Edward's family was something they should do, unfortunately, but maybe not at the expense of canceling Christmas with an elderly widow. The canceling, of course, would cause Eliza a whole heap of drama that she didn't think she had the energy for. Especially not during Christmas, the supposed pinnacle of family togetherness, non-stop joy, and peace. What a farce that was.

Jacob scoffed. "Don't be such a stick-in-the-mud. We always do the same thing for the holidays, going over to your mother's. We can do something different for a change. See some new people. Have fun."

Eliza bristled at being called a "stick-in-the-mud." She could have reminded Jacob of all the events she wanted to go to with him, but he always declined. He wasn't into author visits, or any of the interesting and free programs going on at their local library. She'd recently shown him a flier they received in the mail about a farm-to-table dinner at a local organic farm. He had looked it over, shrugged and said, "Looks awfully expensive for a bunch of weird vegetables they grew themselves."

Even though he'd been the lead guitarist in a local band when they met, he usually didn't want to go to the same concerts Eliza would like to see. So they'd gotten into a habit of not doing much. Well, not much recreational. They were always going to work. And helping her mother. And getting the kids through high school. And taking care of their house and yard. And on and on and on.

Jacob took Eliza's lack of a verbal response as being enthusiastically on board and the matter closed. He turned to go, but then stopped and dropped another bombshell.

"Did you want me to get carryout for dinner?"

"No," Eliza said, opening the drain with her toe so the water could start emptying out of the tub. Suddenly, she wasn't in the mood for a bath anymore. "I asked the kids to make something."

"Uh, yeah. They just locked themselves in their rooms with their phones. They're not cooking anything."

At seventeen and fifteen, Eliza had dreamed her children would be more productive parts of the household, but that hadn't materialized yet. She didn't know where she'd gone wrong or how to help them feel more ownership over the household. From what she'd heard her colleagues say at work, her kids weren't an anomaly, but it didn't soothe her nerves any. Were they destined to live in her basement until she and Jacob died or would a work-ethic and motivation suddenly appear out of thin air? It was just one of many things that popped into her head when insomnia woke her at 3:00 a.m.

There she went. Off on another panic spiral when she already had to break the news to her mother about Christmas. Then start managing everything for the trip.

"Can't you tell them to boil some noodles for pasta?" Eliza's voice sounded shrill to her own ears, but didn't seem to worry Jacob.

"Nah. They'll never do it. I'll just order a pizza. Enjoy the rest of your bath."

"But how will they learn to—"

She might as well have not said anything else. Jacob disappeared from the room, closing the door behind him. Her fluffy purple bathrobe hanging on the back of it looked just as slumped and lifeless as she felt.

Jacob hadn't even noticed that she'd started draining the tub. It made her wonder if anyone in her life really noticed anything she did. Maybe they just noticed what she didn't do...if it was something they expected of her.

As she watched the suds gurgle down the drain, she felt the coil of stress in her core tighten. Everyday she felt one step closer to blowing up. Would she be able to continue holding herself together until after Christmas? For the first time, she was worried that the answer might actually be "no."

❦

"HELLO,   DEAR!"   ELIZA'S   MOTHER   ANSWERED
brightly. "Are you all set for Christmas?"

Not anymore, but Eliza couldn't say that.

"Well, that's actually why I'm calling you." She tried
hard to mask the anxious trepidation in her voice.

"Do you need Great-Grandma's recipe for the apple
raisin stuffing?"

"No. I have that, thanks." Eliza took a deep breath
and decided she just had to rip the bandage off and let
everything fall apart from there.

"Listen, Jacob just told me that his brother invited
us to stay with them over Christmas."

Eliza's mom laughed.

"That's a little last minute don't you think? Too bad.
You've already got plans."

Eliza closed her eyes and rubbed her forehead. This
was going to go even worse than she'd imagined.

It wasn't a whole lot of notice. Her mom was right
about that, but it was a good three weeks, so not
completely out of the question. Well, it was out of the
question for Eliza, but not Jacob, who was inexplicably
giddy to spend a week in the viper's nest.

"That's the thing, Mom. Jacob was so excited they
asked that he told them we'd come."

Eliza could hear her mom huff through the phone.

"You're already coming to my house. We made plans
together first. That's that."

Although Eliza didn't think her mother had

anything awful like dementia, she had noticed that things had become black and white for her mother in a way that didn't fit the reality of Eliza's life. If only things worked out that plainly, then she wouldn't have messes like this to clean up in the first place.

Sure, in a simple world, Jacob would have told his brother they were going to Eliza's mother's on Christmas day and that would be that. But there was also the little matter that they did see Eliza's mother all the time. Edward rarely invited his brother to anything, and despite the fact that they had little in common and weren't particularly close, Jacob was always eager to please Edward. Dynamics like that led Eliza into uncomfortable situations like this, with an elderly mother who didn't give a hoot about compromise anymore. She wanted what she wanted, when she wanted it, damn it! Eliza had been bearing the brunt of those wants since her father passed away eight years ago. Some days it was impossible to please both her mother and her husband, this being one of those times.

She tried again.

"It's very important to Jacob that we go see his brother. Edward doesn't ask him to do anything very often and we haven't really seen them since Derby was born. That's already three years—"

"What do they think your mother is supposed to do? Sit home all alone on Christmas day?"

Eliza knew for a fact they didn't think about her mother at all. Why would they? Besides, Edward and Jacob's own parents weren't going to be around for Christmas because they'd booked themselves a South American cruise with their best friends. Jacob's parents were like that. They married crazy young and had Edward when Jacob's mom was only nineteen. Unlike Eliza's mom, Jacob's parents had stayed active and enjoyed outdoor activities like golfing together, gardening, and they even hit the gym regularly. All of this meant they were only in their late sixties and still having the time of their lives, whereas Eliza's mom had always been a homebody who preferred crafty, sedentary activities, which she'd long given up when her arthritis kicked in. She'd laugh you out of the house, with a list of errands in your hand, if you even mentioned her doing something like taking a seniors cruise.

"Jacob's parents are on a cruise with their friends. They won't be back until after New Year's so I'm sure they expect that you'd be doing something like that too."

"Well I'm certainly not doing that. I'm expecting to celebrate the holiday with my only family. You're abandoning your elderly mother for Christmas?"

Eliza's left eye started twitching and a dull pain pulsed behind her eyebrow. Many recent conversations with her mother left her with these symptoms. In her own head, Eliza referred to it as "the mom effect." She couldn't say so to anyone though. Jacob would tell her the fix was easy: stop talking to her mother so much. As if that was an option. If she told anyone else they'd think she was a stone cold bitch. A couple of her coworkers had already lost their mothers and Eliza knew they'd switch with her in a heartbeat if they could have one more day with their moms. But conversations like this made it very difficult to count her lucky stars, as she felt herself being ripped in two directions with the added bonus of a metric ton of guilt pulling her down. How many directions could one person be stretched before they totally broke apart? At this rate, it wouldn't be much longer before Eliza found the definitive answer.

"Mom," Eliza sighed as the pulsing behind her eyebrow got stronger. "I don't want to go either, but it's one of those compromises I have to make in my marriage—"

"Sure. I see. Your own mother means nothing. That's fine. I'll just sit alone on Christmas while my own family runs off to do God knows what."

Now a new emotion was getting into the mix: anger.

"It's not God knows what. It's visiting Jacob's family. He has a right to see his family."

"But *I* don't have a right to see *my* family?"

"Mom!" Eliza was totally exasperated now. The frustration she was trying so hard to suppress came frothing up to the surface. "We just had you over for Thanksgiving two weeks ago and I came over to visit last week. You can't act like we don't ever see you."

"But this is Christmas! The number one day for your family!"

Maybe it was the sudden mood swings of perimenopause, paired with the unfairness of the situation, and a desperate wondering when Eliza could live her own life as an autonomous adult, but she felt a dangerous magma of rage rise in her stomach.

"Edward and Dymond are family! The other side of my family with Jacob. I'm sorry you don't like it, but there's only one of me, and only one Christmas day. I can't split myself up between everyone who would like to see me. We can do Christmas at your house before or after Christmas day. It isn't the end of the world."

It felt like the end of the world. There was more than enough angst and drama for the end of everything. It would probably be less upsetting if a huge fireball did come out of the sky and put an end to all this petty arguing and planning and frustration.

"Well, why didn't you just say that? You can come to my house before you leave and we can do Christmas first."

Eliza wanted to scream and throw her phone across the room. Before they left? One more thing she had to take care of before the trip. If anyone asked her, (they wouldn't), she'd say that she wanted to skip Christmas this year and just stay home in her pajamas. No formal dinner. No formal meals at all. How glorious would it be if everyone just grazed and ate something when they were hungry? A day of everyone taking care of themselves for a change. What a dream that would be!

Instead of blowing up, she bottled it up, pushed the rising magma down, and went for her exit strategy.

"Great. Yeah, I should have just said that. Silly me. Anyway, I gotta get dinner going. I'll call you later and we can figure out what day we can do Christmas. Ok?"

"Sounds good. Have a good day, dear. Oh, and Eliza?"

Eliza's heart clenched.

"Yeah?"

"Don't get so worked up about things. It isn't good for your heart." Her mother chuckled and hung up.

Eliza ended the call feeling like she had whiplash,

had survived being beaten up, and a tiny sliver of relief that she'd done what she'd intended with the call. Jacob would never understand the toll it took for her to have this conversation with her mother so they could follow his joy and go to Edward's house. There was no Christmas present big enough to balance this level of mother management. And that was only the first step done. She still had to deal with packing, figuring out presents for Edward and his family, getting the house in order, finding someone to care for the dog while they were out of town. And not forget to squeeze in some time to do a bonus Christmas with her mother. None of that even took into account that Eliza and Jacob both had their jobs for the next couple weeks before Christmas. It wasn't Christmas break yet. Even the "break" wouldn't be a break because she'd be wearing the masks of happy mother/wife/sister-in-law/aunt and walking on eggshells to fit into Edward and Dymond's ridiculous life.

She found that her heart was pounding in her chest. Was it perimenopause symptoms or was the big one finally coming for her after all that stress? Each option was equally plausible.

Eliza switched her phone to silent and put it on her dresser. In the meantime, she would give herself a five-minute break to sit on her bed, head in hands, and maybe cry before moving on to the next task of her day, and the next, and so on, until she could finally crawl into bed for the night and then do it all again in the morning.

BY THE TIME THEY WERE STUFFING THE LUGGAGE into their Chevy Trailblazer, Eliza fantasized about slipping on their liberally salted driveway and snapping her ankle just so she could sit out this "most wonderful" holiday. She couldn't dare voice such feelings to anyone, let alone Jacob, who would say she was being dramatic and negative. He wouldn't say it to be malicious. He would think he was rallying her, but in her very few quiet moments, she knew there was increasingly less to rally. She had never imagined herself as someone who would buckle under the weight of being in the "sandwich generation," but her mother and daughter sides were unraveling at an alarming rate. Eliza put in a daily Herculean effort to not let it show, but she was slipping. Even if she was the only one who noticed.

It was all so exhausting and with each revolution of the tires on the expressway to her brother-in-law's home, her hopes of reclaiming any Christmas cheer grew dimmer.

"Honey, why don't you put on some Christmas music? We should be there in less than an hour. Just enough time to get everyone in the holiday mood."

Oh, Jacob. He should know better by now. After all, he'd lived alongside her these past two decades. They'd both had their share of arguments with the two teens in the backseat who had seemingly turned into angry aliens overnight. From what Eliza could glean from information online and from the personal anecdotes of her co-workers, Bella, age seventeen, had possibly five to seven more years of parental resentment before she came back around to thinking they might know something. Bobby, at fifteen, was just getting started. A little

Christmas music sing-song wasn't going to work the magic it might have when they were a few years younger.

Still, she was trying not to hate every minute of this stupid trip. Or, more accurately, she was trying not to let it show that she hated every minute of this stupid trip. She wasn't in the mood to listen to the sappy nostalgia of Christmas music, but if that's what it would take to get Jacob to shut up about how delightful this all was, then so be it.

She opened her music app to find her Christmas favorites playlist, which heavily featured Kelly Clarkson, Bing Crosby, and Michael Bublé. Then she navigated to her playlists, scrolled until she found "Christmas," hit a button, dismissed a weird error, and waited for the tunes to begin.

The car remained silent.

"Sure, everyone go ahead and ignore me," Jacob said peevishly. "It's not like it's Christmas Eve or anything."

Eliza was already on edge, but this rankled her even more. She didn't have a teammate to head into the holiday fray with. She was the lone defector and it wasn't a great feeling.

"I did put it on. Maybe my phone isn't synced up with the radio properly?"

Jacob went through the string of voice commands that confirmed her phone was connected to the audio system. Eliza looked back at her music app and discovered that the Christmas playlist was no longer there. Her heart dropped into her stomach as the fear of losing her mind, which had become so familiar these past few months, caused her to panic.

"It was right here!" she exclaimed. "I just clicked on it and now it's gone."

"What do you mean 'it's gone?'" Jacob asked, an edge to his voice. "You can't just misplace a playlist on your phone. That's ridiculous."

She felt her cheeks heat in embarrassment. She wasn't so incompetent that she couldn't use her own smartphone anymore. This was the sort of thing that happened to her mother, not her. There had to be a logical explanation. She must be looking right at it and not seeing it, which was another thing that seemed to be happening more frequently. It was just a peri-menopause moment, but it didn't make it any less alarming.

"Bella!" she shouted, figuring that if she couldn't get her brain in line at the moment, she could defer to her daughter.

Bella was engrossed in whatever she was listening to with her earbuds, so Eliza had to call her a couple more times to get her attention.

Finally, Bella popped out one earbud. "What?" she asked in that special way annoyed teenagers do.

"I can't find my Christmas playlist. Can you see where it is?" She offered the phone to Bella, who sighed and took it. After scrolling around for a few minutes, Bella passed the phone back up.

"Well?" Eliza asked, exasperated.

"Looks like you deleted it," Bella said matter-of-factly and replaced her earbud to distance herself from the foolishness all around her.

Of course, now that Bella said it, Eliza's brain cleared up and the weird error message she'd dismissed was served up as a clear memory. It wasn't a weird error at all, but confirmation that she wanted to delete the playlist, and all its tracks, from her phone. Why did she understand what it was now that the damage was done, but it didn't even register in the moment? Day by day it was getting harder to hold body and mind together. Eliza didn't know how she was going to survive until she'd finally made it through menopause, whenever that magical day might come. She was tired of holding on so tightly and the sensation of slipping grew stronger all the time.

"Geez Eliza, if you didn't want to play it you could have just said so." Jacob had a teasing lilt to his voice, but Eliza wasn't in the mood to be teased. The increasing frequency of her ludicrous mishaps made good jokes for everyone else, but it was another thing entirely to feel at odds with her own body and mind. How could she have done something so stupid? It wasn't like she'd never used a music playlist on her phone before. She did it all the time. Even though she hadn't wanted to listen to them at the moment, they were her favorite Christmas songs. She'd like to listen another time, but they were gone. She'd have to purchase them again. What a waste of time and money. There was no telling if her foggy brain would even remember all the songs she'd had.

As tears started to flood her eyes, no doubt courtesy of her roller coaster hormones, her phone pinged with her mother's assigned text sound.

Annoyance dried up her tears before they could spill onto her cheeks. For goodness' sake, she couldn't even feel sorry for herself for sixty seconds before another issue needed her attention. She was beginning to think Ebenezer Scrooge was onto something with his "bah humbug" approach to the holidays. It was definitely hard to feel charitable when she couldn't get a moment's rest.

Eliza swallowed the sudden urge to scream and instead looked at the screen. She knew her mother would spiral into chaos if ignored. With her father gone, there was no one in the house to occupy her mother's time and attention. It had all turned to Eliza. If she didn't answer within a few moments, her mother might start to worry, or ruminate on what could possibly be going on that would make Eliza unable to respond to her. She never seemed to consider that Eliza was busy living her own hectic life. As a result, Eliza had learned it was best to answer as soon as she possibly could, whether she was in the mood to communicate or not. Didn't do much for her own nerves, but who cared about those?

Where are you?

Eliza closed her eyes for a moment, as if she could escape to a mythical place where she was in control of her own time. During that calming moment, another text came through.

Is it snowing?

Be careful!

Where are you?

Yep. The chaos spiral had begun.

Eliza got to texting before the interrogation got any more heated.

> Still driving. Everyone's ok. No snow.

> You're not texting and driving are you?

There was no point trying to stop the sarcastic thoughts that filled Eliza's mind with nearly every inter-action she had these days. She was forty-eight years old for goodness' sake. Not texting and driving was some-thing she had to hammer into her own kids...who were risk-loving minors with underdeveloped frontal lobes.

> Why aren't you answering me?

Nevermind the fact that if she actually were driving, she shouldn't be answering her mother at all. Logic didn't hold up anymore. Eliza had a tab of her brain open about eighty percent of the time for worrying about her mother. This was in the background of the ninety-seven percent devoted to worrying about the kids.

> Jacob's driving. Road noise makes it hard to hear my phone. Sorry.

> Are the roads bad?

> We haven't hit any snow. Smooth sailing.

What are the kids doing? Did they
bring books for the ride?

No. They had not brought books for the ride. They
hadn't read a book for fun since they'd finally gotten
their coveted phones, which had sucked them in and
never let them back out. But sometimes it was just
easier to let her mom live in fantasyland than start an
argument about reality.

Yep. They're quiet in the backseat.

Eliza saw more of the dots on her screen indicating
that this conversation wasn't over yet.

Tell me when you get there so I know
you're ok.

Yep. Talk later.

Conversation over for the time being, she stuffed
her phone into her purse and hoped she wouldn't have
to think about it again for a long time.

She tried to stretch her legs out as far as she could
while inside a vehicle. She was tired and sore from being
in the car for hours, heading toward people she didn't
want to be with, for a holiday that felt like a prison
sentence.

"Who's getting excited?" Jacob's voice was annoy-
ingly chipper.

Another tiny piece of Eliza's spirit shriveled up and
died, never to be revived. No. Excitement was certainly

not on the menu for this holiday experience, but she had foreboding and dread in spades.

It seemed like she'd only just started to recover from the debacle that was Thanksgiving when Christmas staggered onto the scene like a bombastic visitor who didn't know when to call it a night. The holiday season was a brutal and relentless beast.

"Five miles to go until our exit! We'll be there before you know it!" Jacob was like Clark Griswold from National Lampoon's Christmas Vacation getting stupidly excited about his light display.

Eliza side-eyed her husband from the passenger seat. She had no idea what was making him so giddy when all she could imagine was Derby running around destroying things for a week straight, while Edward bragged about money and vacations, and Dymond pouted at her phone to make every second Insta-worthy.

Bella and Bobby had their earbuds firmly in place since they'd entered the vehicle hours before. It was a wonder their eyes hadn't permanently dried out and crumbled to dust from staring at their phones the whole way. They hadn't heard a word their father said, nor would they care if they had. Family events weren't the definition of excitement for most teenagers of any generation, and certainly not for these two.

The silence answering Jacob's question stretched on, but Eliza couldn't bear to respond. It wasn't a secret to Jacob that Eliza was no fan of Dymond's. Not that she'd been besties with Edward's first wife either, but at least Michelle had spoken regular English, not the social media jargon gibberish Dymond used. Eliza didn't understand half the things Dymond talked about, nor did she care. She had real life to deal with. Who had time to worry about curating a fake visual guide to their lives for strangers on an app?

"Don't all shout at once," Jacob said, the sarcasm dripping thicker than gloppy pancake batter. "It's Christmastime, for goodness' sake. What's wrong with you sad sacks?"

Eliza couldn't begin to chronicle everything that was wrong with her. She hadn't expected to take stock of herself so thoroughly once she entered her forties, but that's what she'd slowly been doing since the big 4-0 had come and gone. She wouldn't necessarily say it was something "wrong" with her, but she clearly knew that she had zero enthusiasm for spending time with people she didn't care for. On a normal, run-of-the-mill day it was bad enough, but on Christmas, a holiday the entire culture hyped as the shiniest, happiest, most magical day of your year, it was even worse. The expectation for perfection was a thousand ton boulder around her neck. She should adore every family member she encountered. She must be a beacon of hospitality and grace. Her patience and good humor should outshine that of any saint. And not only that, she should cherish absolutely every magical moment because children grow quickly, the elderly pass away, etc., etc. Nobody ever says that middle-aged moms grow weary and disillusioned and just want to sit at home in their pajamas and eat chocolate chip cookies for breakfast. Now that was a holiday fantasy she could get behind. Add a soothing cup of tea and a holiday romance novel and she'd definitely have some enthusiasm.

"No one's even going to speak to me?"

Eliza felt the ever present knot of tension in her chest squeeze a little tighter. He wasn't going to let this go? What was wrong with *him*? Instead, she pushed down her annoyance and rubbed a hand over the crease she'd unwittingly put into her forehead.

"It's been a long car ride, honey. I think we're all a little tired and cranky from that."

Jacob snorted. "That's all behind us now. We're almost to Edward's place. We'll be able to stretch out and relax soon enough."

Relax? Relax! It was all Eliza could do not to break into maniacal laughter. Who would be relaxing? She'd be tiptoeing around every minute, masking how uncomfortable she felt, until she finally got back to her own home.

"Maybe you could tell us what you're most excited for to help get us in the mood." She had no idea where she'd pulled that suggestion from. After seventeen years of motherhood, she'd learned a thing or two about BSing. But that was a particularly good save if she did say so herself. She didn't even sound a little bit patronizing. She was crushing those holiday expectations, even if she was also crushing herself in the process.

She saw Jacob sit a little taller as he finally revealed what he was so damn excited about.

"Eggnog, for one thing. And Edward told me he has a new ninety-eight inch flat screen, high definition television with a whole sound system and theater seating!"

Ah. There it was. Television. Nothing said the joy of holiday togetherness like keeping your eyes glued to a screen the whole time. Although, if she were being honest, given Edward and Dymond's conversation skills, television was about the only viable way to get through the excruciatingly long moments.

"Wow," Eliza said flatly. "That sounds like quite the home theater."

"It's going to be amazing for watching the game!"

Eliza didn't know what game he might be referring to, or even which sport. Her spirit sank lower. So they might be watching a lot of TV, but now it had to be sports related? Maybe she could offer to run to the store for a last minute Poinsettia or candy canes and never come back.

The next thing Eliza knew, they were pulling into the tree-lined driveway of Edward and Dymond's home. It was a 6,800 square foot Instagrammer's paradise on five acres in Cincinnati, Ohio. Eliza knew exactly how much the house cost, since Edward wasn't shy about telling anyone who would listen, and the sum made her eyes water. For that amount, Bella and Bobby could each attend prestigious universities and have money left over. It was a gorgeous six bedroom home, but Eliza couldn't help but think it was totally over the top for a family of three.

The only reason they'd managed to afford such a home, on the heels of Edward's divorce no less, was that Dymond could afford to be an influencer thanks to her great grandfather. He'd started Lafaye Sodas in the early 1900s and it had become a booming regional soda pop company. Some people were born lucky. Others got lucky by knocking up a young soda pop heiress.

Jacob pulled up to the detached three car garage, not to be confused with the attached two car garage, and turned off the engine. Eliza wasn't entirely sure if she was imagining things now, but Jacob may or may not have rubbed his hands together in misplaced glee. For what? Just for watching TV with these people?

She wondered what had happened to the Jacob she'd married all those years ago. For that matter, what happened to the woman she used to be? God knows she hadn't turned into what she'd expected either. That young woman would never have believed she'd become this bitter Scrooge who was actively trying to summon the strength to open the car door and step outside. It wasn't a given that she'd be able to do it, either.

Jacob didn't have any trouble though. He threw his door open and leapt out like a kid at Christmas while the teens in the back blinked back to the real world as they temporarily disconnected from their constant virtual lives.

Heavy. The word hit Eliza as she struggled to motivate herself to get out and put on the holiday act she was expected to perform. That's how she felt...heavy. In mind, body, and spirit. Like she was carrying around the dead weight of the person she used to be, the reality of who she really was, and the ever increasing boulder of who everyone wanted her to be. The roles she had to play were layering on top of her as she struggled to unbuckle her seatbelt. Adoring wife - gleefully putting aside her misgivings to give her husband the Christmas he inexplicably wanted. Gentle and endlessly patient mother - even though the kids wanted her to back off and shut up, they also wanted her to know exactly what they wanted to eat and when and have it ready for them...and clean up their messes, physical and emotional...and be the butt of their jokes, and their punching bag, and their champion but always on their own terms. Cheerful sister-in-law - to two people who knew and cared nothing about who she was and what she was interested in. But she did have to soak up everything Edward and Dymond cared about and were interested in and nod and "ooh" at all the right parts. Attentive and dutiful daughter - even though her mother was not at Edward and Dymond's house, she'd still expect Eliza to answer her every text within seconds. Doting aunt - it wasn't Derby's fault he was overstimulated and spoiled, but Eliza must bite her tongue at his unruly behavior and pretend he was just the sweetest angel she'd ever laid eyes on, her own children included. Authentic self - no. That role hadn't been cast in this performance. Strangely enough, it never was. Eliza doubted she'd even know how to play it anymore, if she ever had.

Eliza realized that even the kids had dragged themselves out of the vehicle and were stretching outside their doors. She couldn't hide from it any longer.

As if moving in a stranger's body, she watched her hand pull the door latch and saw her leg move out of the car. The cold air did nothing to welcome her, nor did it stir her to a sense of action or purpose. Thoughts of hibernation came to mind. Wouldn't it be lovely if she could just snuggle into a den of her favorite shearling fleece blankets and close her eyes for the next week? At the end of it all, she could open them and be in her own house, but a different version. In this version, she would have the time and energy to pursue a few things that interested her. She'd have downtime to recharge and reconnect with herself and her changing body. She wouldn't be interrupted by her mother all the time. The kids would help out when she asked. She and Jacob would be on the same page more often. A dreamy smile spread over her face at this glowing beacon of a false reality.

"Here," Jacob thrust a garbage bag full of presents at Eliza. Her arms automatically encircled it. "You can bring the presents in, me and the kids will bring the rest of the stuff."

The kids groaned and Eliza snapped out of her wildly fictitious daydream. It was only right that she carried the gifts. She was the one who'd picked out and purchased all of them. No small feat to get something appropriately nice and vaguely intimate for people who had a considerably higher income and bought everything their whims desired.

Her legs started walking her to the front door even though her mind rebelled with every step. The dreamy smile she'd had just moments before transformed into a realistic but fake version of a happy holiday smile. She willed a sparkle into her eyes to match the occasion. No one would ever accuse her of having a smile that didn't reach her eyes. After twenty years of marriage, convincing fake smiles were a superpower of hers.

She marched right up to the front door, each step moving her more firmly into the setting of the roles she was playing: benevolent mother, adoring wife, humble sister-in-law, Christmas elf.

She balanced the bag on her knee to free a hand to ring the doorbell, even though she knew full well their hosts were aware they'd arrived. She also knew that it wouldn't do to throw open the doors before the bell had been rung. They may be family, but they definitely weren't close enough for that.

Derby started screaming inside as soon as the doorbell chime faded away and Eliza turned up the intensity on her sparkling eyes. She stared squarely at the aromatic pine wreath on the door, daring its shimmery gold ribbon to outshine her smile.

She heard footsteps getting closer, the lock disengage, and then there was Dymond's glowing face. What a picture she was! She pulled the door open completely so Eliza could get hit with the full effect of her appearance. Dymond was in full makeup as if they were about to embark on a night on the town, rather than a family holiday at home. Her eyelids had a glittery shimmer to them, which was nearly overshadowed by her outrageous fake lashes. It looked like she'd had her hair done as well. Her perfect bottle blonde hair fell in gentle waves all around her head.

Her young body had bounced back from childbirth, in part due to her rigorous Pilates regimen. She looked like she belonged in a Hallmark Christmas movie with her winter white scoop neck sweater with three quarter sleeves that sounds simple, but looked glamorous. She'd paired it with burgundy pants that must have been tailored because they fit her like a dream. Even though she was hosting a family gathering in her own home, she wore a pair of white heels embellished with diamond accents. Her perfect neck was bare but her wrists were adorned with sparkling bangles. Her generous engagement and wedding rings twinkled as she waved her hands in excitement over her guests' arrival.

The hallway behind her flickered with soft candlelight and as Eliza stepped over the threshold, she was enveloped with the scent of cinnamon and vanilla. The candley kind of scent, not actual cooking. It was homey in the way a home goods store might be. Beautiful to behold, but the soul was missing.

"Merry Christmas, Eliza!" Dymond exclaimed, opening her arms in a "ta da" manner because no one was going in for a hug. For one thing, Eliza was hugging a bag of presents already, but part of the act was that she'd just stepped lightly into the house looking as flawless as sister-in-law 2.0.

"Merry Christmas!" Eliza echoed, her voice as fake sparkly as her eyes.

While Eliza was not competing with a beautiful woman in her mid-twenties, she couldn't help but feel the loss of her own youth. She used to look as good as Dymond. Now, she felt the expanded butt, thighs, and stomach her aging body had gifted her. She'd been in the car for hours so there was no way she would arrive put together like Dymond, but whereas the younger woman looked ready to step into a photo shoot, Eliza felt that her look must exude "ready to collapse into bed." She'd opted for stretchy black leggings, since she couldn't very well show up in sweatpants. Her footwear was waterproof snow boots that she'd need to kick off before leaving the doorway area. She didn't do designer anything and was bundled up in a generic black puffer jacket. Underneath, she'd reveal a green tunic sweater that covered her butt, and a costume jewelry wreath brooch that had been her grandmother's. Her hair? She didn't bother with hair dye and the grays, more accurately, the whites, were sprinkling in from her temples. That didn't bother her though. She was what she was and she wanted to know what her actual self looked like. No shade to Dymond for choosing the bottle blonde. It was just too much hassle, and money, for Eliza to deal with. There were no gentle waves on her head. It was probably flat as a board, with a top layer of frizzies. Try as she may, the frizzies never seemed to smooth. She'd come to grips with that, too.

Finally, the doorway behind her filled with her husband and children.

"Merry Christmas!" Jacob exclaimed while stepping onto the welcome mat.

"Merry Christmas," the teens mumbled behind him.

Edward appeared in the hallway with Derby tucked under one arm, legs kicking in the air, while the front end continued to emit a shrill howl.

"Hey guys!" Edward hollered over the din. "Glad you made it. Come on in."

"Wet shoes stay by the door!" Dymond said in an apologetic, sing-song voice as if Eliza and her oafish family would dare to track wet boots over the hardwood floors.

"Look," Edward tried to appease his wailing son. "Bella and Bobby are here."

"I hate Bella and Bobby!" Derby shouted back.

Dymond made a frowny face and affected the baby talk tone she often took with Derby. "Now Derby, dat's not a nice fing to say to your cousins. Dey came all the way here to see you!"

Derby started flailing anew in Edward's arm, resulting in Edward giving up and putting him down.

The unhappy child turned and ran back from whence he'd come, screaming all the way.

Eliza chanced a quick glance at her kids. They were looking at each other with wicked teenage glee. What could be more cringe-worthy than a greeting like that from a preschooler? Cringey for Derby, of course. Not for them.

Dymond turned back to her guests without a trace of embarrassment. "He'll warm up."

Indeed.

Since no one offered to take the unwieldy present bag from her, Eliza set it on the floor next to the doormat so she could unlace her boots and take them off.

There was not so much as a smudge of salt on Dymond and Edward's gleaming floor. She wasn't going to be the one to sully it.

Eventually, everyone got into the house, out of their coats and boots, and had taken their luggage into their rooms.

There were four guest rooms. As they walked down the hall past the unused guest room, Eliza felt a little pang of longing. It might actually be pleasant if she had her own room to retreat to during all of this. Jacob would complain, of course, but man, some space from all of these people would be glorious. That daydream fizzled away once Jacob shut the door behind them in their room.

As little as Eliza could relate to Dymond, she had to admit the woman knew how to decorate a space. Their guest room was like a travel brochure come to life. They had a king bed with a forest green and white plaid bedspread. The headboard was mostly concealed by an assortment of aesthetically pleasing pillows with either green, white, or black cases. The hardwood floors were throughout the house, which required the use of lots of plushy rugs. There was a fluffy white rug on both sides of the bed, so bare toes would never have to meet cold wood.

The walnut bedside tables were adorned with woven off-white runners, a brass lamp, and a green, pine scented jar candle on each.

It was a cozy space without a hint of clutter anywhere. Even though it was a guest room, it gave the impression that it just sat around looking pretty, whether anyone was there to view it or not.

Jacob plopped the suitcases down on the foot of the bed, yawned, and scratched his belly.

"Isn't this great, El?"

"Mmm."

"This bed's bigger than ours. We can really get up to something with all this room." He patted the foot of the bed and waggled his eyebrows suggestively.

A frown tugged down the corners of Eliza's mouth. Being in a house with her brother-in-law, his young adult bride, and their screaming child was one of the least arousing settings she could think of.

She wasn't that familiar with the layout of the house. Derby's room might be just below theirs. Or, worse, Edward and Dymond's. Who wanted to be boinking in a room surrounded by family? Who wanted to be boinking at all?

Eliza couldn't even remember the days when physical intimacy was the natural extension of emotional and mental intimacy. They were running around so much, tackling different errands and taking care of different problems that when they found time together, all she wanted was a deep conversation and a soothing cuddle. Jacob, on the other hand, was often too tired to talk. Then they'd crawl into bed at the end of a long, frustrating day and she'd be surprised and dismayed to find his hand grabbing her breast or sliding between her legs. Too exhausted for mental stimulation, but he was more than virile enough for physical exertion. Eliza felt just the opposite. With little deep emotional connection during her days, the last thing she had energy for was sex. Not only that, but her changing body had decided it should take far longer to get in the mood than it ever had before. While one half of her brain pondered whether to be aroused or exhausted, the other half would calculate how many hours of sleep she might be able to get if she did try to play along. If she would even fall asleep afterwards. It used to be a given that both of them would sleep well after a good romp in bed. Now, Jacob would be snoring right away as he always had, but Eliza would find herself just listening to him sleep while wishing she could do the same.

While all this was going through Eliza's mind, making her feel even worse, Jacob was completely oblivious and really getting into the idea of making use of the big bed.

"What do you say?" he asked, flirty grin on his face. "We could have a quickie right now before we even go back downstairs. Wouldn't that be fun?"

Eliza could practically feel the cortisol coursing through her system. It still hadn't faded from the long drive and the letdown of sharing a home with people she didn't like. Stress was almost constantly her top setting and it couldn't be switched off by a pinch on the derrière or a lusty look from Jacob. It might have been enough in her twenties, possibly her thirties, but things were different now. She hated feeling like a wet blanket, but that just added to her stress. Here was another thing she wasn't performing up to expectations. Stressing about her waning libido made it even harder to get in the mood.

There was nothing arousing about being in her in-laws' home, but even if there was, the logistical tabs of her brain were already opening up. First, they'd have to disrobe and once she took off her traveling clothes, she wouldn't want to put them on again. Although it wasn't necessarily weird to change after a journey, she didn't want to draw attention to herself for that. And Jacob didn't understand that she wouldn't actually be in the mood at the drop of a hat. To honestly have it be enjoyable for both of them, it was going to take time they didn't have. Then there was the act itself. What if the bed squeaked? What if Dymond or Edward knocked on the door in the middle of it? Jacob couldn't finish without falling asleep instantly, so then what? He was just going to take a nap and she would have to awkwardly go back downstairs to mingle? They'd both have to shower because she certainly wasn't going to slap on her used clothes and parade around smelling of sweat and sex in front of her children and in-laws. Why didn't Jacob consider any of these things?

"Settle down," Eliza said. "We have to get back downstairs and be sociable. Besides, it's rude to get here and just disappear into our rooms. Why bother coming here if we just wanted to be alone?"

Her words didn't diminish Jacob's heavy-lidded look. "Who cares? Besides, that's the point of a quickie, it's quick. Won't even take more than ten minutes. You can think of it as an early Christmas present."

A gift for him or her...she didn't have to wonder.

Luckily, she didn't have to assess the path of least resistance, to deny or acquiesce, because their conversation was interrupted by a knock on the door. She felt a little vindicated that one of the possible problems she'd foreseen was valid, but it wasn't enough to lighten her mood.

Eliza flashed a look at Jacob. "See?" it meant to convey. "It's not like we're alone here."

He groaned.

"Hey guys," Edward's voice drifted through the closed door. "Dymond's been dying to try out our new bar. We've got pretty much anything. What do you want to drink? She'll make it while you're putting your stuff away."

Eliza stiffened. She hadn't known about the new home bar. Of course they had it well stocked. Eliza's attempt at a thoughtful gift for them was a bottle of wine that the store clerk had told her was nice. It had set her back $80, which she thought was a hefty sum for a beverage of any type, but was probably cheap to the likes of Dymond and Edward. Suddenly, the wine didn't seem like such a good idea.

Jacob had an opposite reaction. His eyes widened as he contemplated the world of cocktails within his reach.

"I've been dying for a good eggnog, and don't be light on the rum."

"An eggnog? I would have thought you'd need a grown up drink after that long drive."

Jacob's face clouded at the customary ribbing from his older brother.

"It's Christmastime, man. I've been in the mood for a proper eggnog since Thanksgiving. What's wrong with that?"

"Nothing." Edward did a fake cough to fake conceal his real sentiment, "Weak!"

"Hey!" But Edward was done with his brother and turned his attention to his sister-in-law instead.

"One eggnog for Baby Jake. What would you like, El?"

What she'd really like was something strong enough to knock her out until this whole trip was over, but that wouldn't be playing her holiday role properly.

"What is Dymond going to have?" Eliza asked.

"Oh, she's been on a chocolate martini kick."

"I'll have the same. Thank you."

"You got it. Eggnog and a chocolate martini coming right up."

With his train of thought rerouted by the drink, Jacob opened his suitcase and set to unpacking as fast as possible.

"Finally, a good eggnog. See? Aren't you glad we came?"

"You sure are," Eliza said quietly. Jacob didn't seem to notice.

They put their things away without any more chitchat and made their way into the picturesque living room for drinks and awkward conversation.

Looking around, Eliza couldn't deny that she was dazzled. Dymond set a scene like nobody's business. Probably why her Instagram was so popular.

Entering the room was like entering a themed resort. The huge open room had expansive golden wood floors. The far end from the entryway had a roaring fire in a huge fireplace. Off to the left of the hearth was a massive Christmas tree, easily nine feet tall, color coordinated with red and gold ornaments and white lights. Even the tree skirt was a sparkling gold material.

A long couch sat in the middle of the room, facing the cozy winter scene. To each side of the couch, over-stuffed recliners sat at the ready. All of the furniture was upholstered in pristine white. How they managed to still be white with a three-year-old in the house was a mystery to Eliza.

Along the right wall, Eliza discovered the new bar Edward had mentioned. It was crafted of beautifully carved wood that matched the floors. A swag of holly was perfectly draped across the front and a string of white lights glowed all along the top edge. Dymond stood behind the bar photographing the cocktails she'd finished making.

"Wow!" Jacob exclaimed, not unlike a child opening presents. "This looks awesome!"

He nudged Eliza with his elbow and leaned in. "See? Just like being on vacation."

Perhaps it was, if the vacation involved fake fun and Christmas beauty without any heart.

Eliza and Jacob walked over to the bar to retrieve their photogenic drinks.

"Just a sec," Dymond said, arranging a ball of holly between the glasses. "I'm going to try it with more saturation and a light vignette. Gotta make sure it slaps."

Eliza had no idea what that meant, but she smiled politely. "Of course. Take your time."

"Totes," Dymond agreed as she seriously studied the picture on her phone screen.

Finally, after a few different angles, Dymond seemed satisfied enough to offer the drinks to her guests.

"To Christmas!" Dymond exclaimed, lifting her glass. Eliza and Jacob followed suit, all clinking glasses lightly before taking a sip.

Eliza's chocolate martini tasted like candy with a little punch at the end. This could go down very easily. She'd have to pace herself.

Bella and Bobby shuffled into the room and sat on the couch, a generous cushion width between them. Derby raced in on his pudgy bare feet with two Hot Wheels cars in hand. He dropped to his knees, hard, in front of the couch and got to playing. Bella and Bobby sullenly watched Derby crawl around on the floor and smash his toy cars together with all his strength. "YAW!" he bellowed each time he launched the cars into each other, which was every couple seconds.

Eliza quickly took another sip.

Edward quietly came up behind them and clapped a hand on Jacob's shoulder, causing him to startle and slosh a little of his eggnog onto the floor.

"Gee whiz, Baby Jake," Edward chuckled. "You gotta chill out."

"Hey, sorry," Jacob stammered. "I didn't know you were—"

Edward didn't care what his brother was saying and turned to Dymond instead. "You'll want to towel that off before it ruins the floor."

"Sure thing, babe," Dymond answered and scurried out from behind the bar, towel in hand. She looked far too formal to be crouched on the floor wiping up a tiny spill. Edward was wearing jeans and a flannel shirt. Surely, he could have asked Dymond to toss him the towel so he could clear the mess.

Eliza subconsciously narrowed her eyes at Edward, but no one noticed, since no one was looking at her.

Miniscule mess cleaned, Edward led Jacob off to walk the perimeter of the room and point out all the new and expensive upgrades they'd made to everything.

Since everyone else was at least mildly occupied, Eliza decided to attempt small talk with Dymond.

"The house looks beautiful. I don't know how you do it. There's not a thing out of place."

"Oh, thanks." Dymond held her martini in her hand and vaguely gazed at Derby.

Eliza was at a dead end before they'd even gotten started.

She steeled herself for another try.

"This chocolate martini is delicious. I'm glad I decided to try what you were having. Yummy!" She took another sip for emphasis and strength.

This line of conversation seemed to perk Dymond up a bit.

"Aren't they the best? I found the recipe on Drinkie Dina's Instagram and it looked so good I had to try it for myself." Dymond took another sip, as if to drive home the point.

Apparently, that was the end of the conversation. Dymond did a fine job having one-sided conversations on her Instagram lives all the time, but when it came to conversing with her in-laws, there was far less engagement.

Eliza hadn't been particularly close to Edward's first wife, Michelle, but she'd at least known how to have a polite conversation.

Eliza eyed the overstuffed recliner closest to the Christmas tree that she planned to settle in for the duration, but decided to make one last attempt to talk with Dymond.

"Derby sure is getting big. Are you thinking about preschool?"

He was still violently smashing his cars together and shouting.

"Yes," Dymond agreed. "He's my big little guy, but he doesn't want to potty train."

That was a little hook she could hang a conversation on.

"It happens sooner or later. Bobby wasn't a big fan of the potty at that age either. I remember we were so worried he'd never get the hang of it, but one day, it just clicks."

"I hope so," Dymond said.

A wistful smile crossed Eliza's lips as a memory came to her. "There was this DVD I got from the library one day. I forget the name of it, but it was basically a music video of little kids and potties singing about how great it was to be a big kid and use the potty.

Bobby loved it and it really helped him turn the corner–"

"DVDs!" Dymond exclaimed. "Who even has a DVD player anymore? Potty Mommy on Insta has a list of tips and tricks I've been trying to follow, but Derby just doesn't care. He'd rather kick his potty down the hall than sit on it. Potty Mommy says..."

Eliza didn't care what a person who called herself "Potty Mommy" had to say about potty training. She'd done it twice herself, successfully, but Dymond didn't care about that. Obviously, Eliza was outdated and laughable. Too dull to know anything useful. Had to glam it up on the Gram to be taken seriously.

Eliza let Dymond fizzle out on her Potty Mommy tips and that was it. Eliza gave up. She took another sip of her drink, sort of raised it in an awkward salute to Dymond and made her way to the recliner. It enveloped her as she sat down, but not unpleasantly. It was like a supportive full body hug. In fact, she kind of loved it. She only wished it might smother her completely and save her from this agonizing trip. Alas, it stopped short of asphyxiation.

From her cushy vantage point, she could observe everyone else in the room. Dymond was still hovering near the bar, sipping and watching her son crash his cars together. Bella and Bobby hadn't moved from the couch. They alternated looking at Derby in shock and dismay, and flashing each other loaded glances. At least it made a change from staring at their screens all the time.

Edward and Jacob had completed their turn about the room and had wound up in front of the fireplace.

Edward had assumed a power pose, with his hand on the mantle and a foot on the stone hearth. A man in his domain. Jacob nodded enthusiastically to whatever was being said, but Eliza could only think of Edward's insulting moniker, "Baby Jake." In that moment, she could see what he meant. Edward exuded confidence, while Jacob was more tucked into himself. He looked smaller and less sure than his brother. It was a juxtaposition she only noticed when the two were together. At home, Jacob was a perfectly capable adult male. Once he was around Edward, however, it was like he turned back into the baby brother. Never good enough or cool enough to please Edward. It made Eliza equal parts sad and angry, but it wasn't her problem to fix. Jacob would have to admit it and address it himself, which didn't seem to be likely any time soon.

Eliza sighed and took another sip of her martini. It really did taste like candy. She could knock back quite a few of these if she didn't watch it. She hadn't decided yet if she wanted to watch it or not.

Her phone vibrated in her pocket, reminding her that she hadn't told her mother they'd arrived safely. Shit. She didn't bother her teenagers about their whereabouts as much as her mother demanded to know hers.

She pulled her phone out, wishing she didn't have to be like Pavlov's dog, responding immediately every single time. Her kids did a great job of ignoring her texts. It was irritating, of course, but she could at least appreciate that their brains weren't fully developed. Besides, when she texted them and said, "Are you going to be home for dinner?" and they left her on read, she could passive aggressively not make enough food for everyone. Then she could innocently say, "Well, you didn't tell me you were coming home. I assumed you were grabbing fast food with your friends. Just send me a 'Y' or 'N' next time and there won't be any confusion."

A glance at her phone confirmed her suspicion, although really, who else would text her. It's not like she had any friends or other family who would send her anything. All her other mom friends were in the same boat, being run ragged by their families and their own physical changes. Who had time for girl trips, and drinks after dinner, or even a text? If Eliza wasn't running around all day, she'd probably fall asleep. Unless she'd gone to bed, of course. In which case she could lie awake for hours thinking about everything that ever happened to her, wondering how things were going to turn out for the kids, and how marriage was a hell of a lot different than the happily-ever-after society painted it to be.

Did you get there yet?

Yes we're here. Just settling in. It's rude to be texting.

She knew she shouldn't have added that last part but it was scarcely within her control. Her left eyelid was starting to twitch. Between sitting around in a home she didn't feel comfortable in, and being forced to share a high-pressure holiday with people she didn't have warm feelings for, holding in her frustration was getting more difficult.

> You were supposed to tell me when
> you got there!

As much as she knew it wasn't worth getting upset over, she couldn't help feeling the mounting stress in her body. A volcano had a lot in common with Eliza. Magma and pressure were always stirring beneath the surface. Usually it stayed contained, out of sight where it belonged, but the cracks and fissures were very real. With each additional stressor, the magma rose higher. It was only a matter of time before she blew. It was something she fantasized about. And yet, she knew everyone would be shocked and disappointed that Saint Eliza was actually a normal person with limits and boundaries too. They wouldn't miss the opportunity to let her know that her failure to live up to perfection was unacceptable.

> We just got here and put our stuff
> away.

It was a struggle to resist typing, "Chill out and back off. I'm not a child anymore!"

> I don't know why you couldn't have
> just stayed home.

There it was, the disapproval that she hadn't gotten her way. "Stayed home" was a misnomer. "Come to my house" is what she really meant.

"Who are you texting over there?" Edward interrupted her inner turmoil with a taunting tone. "You got a boy toy we don't know about?" He elbowed Jacob in the ribs and laughed heartily.

Jacob shook his head, as if Edward's obnoxious joke was just a trivial thing to endure. He didn't swat him like a brother could or tell him not to tease his wife like that, so Eliza's magma level rose higher. Not only that, the immense room seemed to shrink around her, squeezing her tighter than the overstuffed chair.

Derby grabbed one of his cars, stood up and smashed it into Bobby's kneecap with all the strength his little preschooler body could muster.

"CRASH!" Derby yelled.

"Ow!" Bobby hollered, instantly grabbing his knee to protect what was left of it and try to soothe the pain.

A new text buzzed on Eliza's phone and...That. Was. It.

The final straw she'd wondered about for years had arrived. The magma boiled up, overflowing her brain with the rage she'd worked for so long to keep down.

"How dare you spew such flagrant bullshit in front of my children!"

Edward's shit-eating grin vaporized instantly under the heat of her wrath, but that small show of her power only made her stronger.

All eyes turned to her, but she didn't feel any embarrassment or shame. She only felt that her moment of vindication had come and she wasn't going to back away from it now.

Eliza struggled her way out of the super plushy chair.

"Lady say bad word!" Derby pointed at her in the accusatory manner that only a young child can.

"You just hurt your cousin, Bobby!" she snapped back. "That's bad! Bad behavior. You don't hit people with toys. How would you like it if Bobby hit you?"

Derby clutched his toy truck to his chest, as if Eliza was going to snatch it out of his hands from across the room.

"Say you're sorry or Santa Claus is going to take away all your toys instead of bringing you new ones."

Derby's eyes grew wide as saucers and his lower lip started to tremble.

"Hey," Dymond said placidly, as if waking from a dream. Eliza turned on her with her newfound uninhibited rage.

"Maybe if you did anything to teach your kid manners, he wouldn't be clocking people with his toys in the first place. You didn't even say anything. I'm not just going to sit here and smile while your kid hurts mine."

Dymond, like everyone else, was speechless.

Eliza turned to Bobby. "Are you ok?"

Bobby stared at his mother as if seeing her for the first time. He answered with a slight shrug.

"Go in the kitchen and wrap some ice in a towel and put it on your knee so it doesn't swell."

He'd never moved so fast when asked to do something. He was up and out of that room like a shot.

Next, Eliza's gaze fell on her daughter. Bella looked mildly terrified rather than her normal snarky bemusement.

"Go help your brother."

Bella also dashed from the room, grateful to have an excuse to flee the horrifying display her mother was putting on.

Edward put his hands up like a criminal. "Geez, El. Can't you take a joke? Now you're going to attack my son and wife? I think you'd better–"

He really should have kept his mouth shut.

"Really, Edward? *Really?* You're going to play this little game after you're the one who knocked up a girl young enough to be your own daughter? You're the one who left your first family and you have the audacity to joke that I'm texting some guy at my family Christmas party? How screwed up are you?"

To his credit, Edward stood wide-eyed, mouth agape, frozen in shock at Eliza's outburst. It made her feel good.

"Eliza, are you feeling ok?" Jacob misguidedly tried to enter the fray.

Knocking back the rest of her martini, she slammed the glass on the end table. Although she put it down harder than she should have, it didn't break.

"Actually, I feel exhausted. I'm going to bed."

As she crossed the room, she detoured in front of Edward and waved her phone in front of his face.

"For your information, my mother is texting me. She's alone for Christmas because we had to come here. I'm too busy taking care of everyone in my damn family to worry about screwing around like you do!"

She felt a primal scream welling up as a nice exclamation point at the end of her outburst but regained enough control to quell it. Instead, she stomped out of the room, literally seeing red.

As she headed through the hallways to get back to her room, she heard Jacob jogging to catch up with her.

"Hey, what is going on? Are you all right?"

The magma wasn't settled yet. Eliza stopped and turned fast to face Jacob. He nearly crashed into her.

"No, I'm not all right. Did you hear how Edward just talked to me? And you stood there without a peep to defend me. You both just pissed me off."

"We both pissed you off? He was joking. That's how Edward is."

"An asshole? Yeah. I know that. That's why I didn't want to come here."

"You can't just make a scene like that. We just got here, and it's Christmas Eve!"

Eliza crossed her arms over her chest.

"Is it Christmas Eve? Thanks for letting me know. I totally forgot."

"Wow. I guess something's really going on here, but you don't have to take it out on Edward and Dymond."

"Edward, your adulterous brother insinuated that I'm having an affair. Are you really going to stand here and say I shouldn't take that out on him? Right. Any other bullshit rules I need to remember to abide by or can I go to bed now?"

"How much did you have to drink?"

The magma threatened to blast upward and outward again.

"Oh, shut up and grow up."

Jacob did a very good impression of a gasping fish out of water, too shocked to say anything more.

"Go check on our kids, too. They can't find their

way around our own kitchen. They probably aren't finding ice or towels here either."

Eliza turned again and continued her brisk walk to their room. No. *Her* room. The idea came to her in pictures rather than words. She saw herself go into her current guest room, grab her suitcase, and hole up in the extra bedroom she'd eyed before. She didn't want to be with anyone. Not Jacob. Not the kids. Not a soul. She had enough of being smothered and starting from that moment, she could not stand it anymore.

Jacob stood, stunned, in the hallway as Eliza walked away, but before she left him to deal with the fallout for a change, she turned back for a moment.

"I'm sleeping in the empty guestroom. Don't any of you come bother me."

The fake twinkle in her eye had been replaced by a steely glint. Jacob didn't mess around with that. He just nodded and headed back to the living room to try to figure out what to do next. Eliza didn't need any input for her next steps. For once, she knew exactly what she was going to do and she was happy about it.

Before she knew it, she'd locked the door of the spare guest room behind her and stared at the bed while her heart rate began to slow down.

Her phone buzzed in her pocket and the magma rose again.

This time, Eliza didn't even bother to read the text because she knew it was just more crap that she didn't have the bandwidth to deal with anymore. She'd snapped. She'd known it would happen and it had happened spectacularly. At the beginning of a trip with her shitty in-laws. What a joy! She hadn't felt this alive in years. Maybe even decades.

She didn't bother to read her mother's latest message before firing off one of her own.

> I'm turning my phone off. I'll talk to you when we get home.

She wasn't bluffing either. She powered down the phone and walked over to the immaculate white night-stand and shoved it in the drawer.

Without the phone in her pocket, she felt a hundred pounds lighter. What was supposed to be a lifeline had become a life-stealer. Maybe she'd cancel her cellular plan altogether when she got home. After all, she'd grown up in the before times, when a person could breathe without being accessible all the damn time. It felt good to be without it. Like the wide world stretched out before her with infinite possibilities. She could forge her own path and no one else's two cents were part of it.

The well-worn cycle of guilt disappeared. Even the little voice in the back of her head that would repeat things like, "You only get one mother" and "You'll be wishing for just one more text once she's gone" was blissfully silent.

She didn't even feel bad about blowing up. A threshold must have been crossed. Perhaps her last fuck had been given and now she was free to explore what-ever interested her for a change. It was a delicious feeling.

With the weight of her world gone from her, she looked around her luxurious room with fresh eyes.

Apparently, Dymond decorated every single room for the season. What a waste of time. But Eliza was drawn to a framed print on the wall. It was an old-timey cover of Charles Dickens's *A Christmas Carol*. It wasn't a particularly appealing picture. A greenish-tinged Ebenezer Scrooge hunched over stacks of brownish yellow coins. The color palette of the whole thing was drab and uninspiring: gray, brown, black, and that sickly green.

Every year, she insisted the family sit down and watch a different film adaptation of the story. There were so many different versions to choose from and always new ones being made. It was one tradition that even two disaffected teenagers could get behind. They hadn't watched it yet this season. She'd been so overwhelmed with the end of term schedule for the kids and preparing for this awful trip that she hadn't found time to select this year's movie. Even though there would be time now, it was a tradition she didn't want to share with Edward, Dymond, and Derby. Especially not now that she'd told them off.

Rather than withering in shame, the memory brought a small smile to her lips. She'd done it. After sacrificing and repressing her whole life in order to keep everyone else comfortable, she'd finally made her real feelings known. Although she was sure there would be fallout of some sort, it hadn't been the end of the world. She was still here and feeling more energized and authentic than ever. Why had she waited so long? Maybe perimenopause did have some perks after all.

"I think you're ready for some visitors."

Eliza snapped to attention. Who'd said that? It wasn't a voice she recognized. No one had knocked on the door.

"Is someone here?" she asked in a small voice. She wasn't scared, just surprised.

"I am. You were just staring at me."

Her eyes darted around the room, trying to figure out how she could have missed a person and then she turned back to the picture of Scrooge and jumped back with a gasp.

He was not sitting at his counting table anymore. He was standing in front of it and staring out at her. Not staring, actually, but blinking and breathing. Maybe that martini was a whole lot stronger than she'd thought.

"Ebenezer Scrooge?" she asked incredulously. "Are you talking to me?"

He waved at her from the picture frame making it clear that he was, indeed, somehow talking to her.

"I am, Eliza, my dear."

Her hand flew to her chest in surprise.

"You even know my name? I better sit down. I guess I definitely had too much to drink."

She perched herself on the edge of the bed but stayed facing the Scrooge picture.

Scrooge chuckled. "I had similar thoughts when Marley first appeared to me, but I assure you, you're quite in control of your faculties."

"Then how on earth am I conversing with a picture in a frame? You have to admit, that isn't rational."

"Sometimes we need a visit from the irrational to put our lives to rights."

It seemed like sage advice to her.

"Am I to believe you, Ebenezer Scrooge, arguably the most famous fictional character of Charles Dickens, has a message for me?"

He drew himself up tall, filling the frame.

"I assure you, I'm no more fictional than you. And I do have a message for you. It's a good thing you're already sitting."

A staticky ripple went up Eliza's spine. It was insane to be conversing with a picture, let alone a picture of Ebenezer Scrooge, but now he had a startling message for her? There was no way to prepare for something so unbelievable.

"Ok. I guess just go ahead and get it over with."

Ebenezer nodded in a businesslike fashion.

"Eliza Skragg, you will be visited by three spirits tonight."

Eliza's heart dropped toward her stomach as if she were on a roller coaster. There was no way she'd heard him correctly. *She* was going to be visited by three spirits? That wasn't even a real thing. That had happened to Scrooge, in a make-believe story. Real human beings didn't have ghostly visitors on Christmas Eve to save their souls from the foul paths they were on.

Eliza gasped. It had felt so good to be rude to Edward. Was this her swift punishment for daring to assert herself? It wasn't fair. She didn't want to go back to being a doormat and bottling up her frustrations. Finally, she'd let loose with her own feelings instead of pandering to others so they'd feel more comfortable. She couldn't go back now. She just couldn't.

"Me? Why? I haven't been a Scrooge, have I? Why would I need to be visited by spirits?"

She waited anxiously, hoping Scrooge would reveal a mix-up. He probably should have been conversing with a different Eliza Skragg in the Netherlands. One who was embezzling from the daycare center she ran even though she desperately hated young children. Surely, that's who needed a spirit visit. Not this Eliza Skragg, spending a tense Christmas with her in-laws in Cincinnati, Ohio.

"It isn't my place to know why, but I can say from experience that they'll bring you hope for a better way to live."

Eliza frowned trying to process what was happening to her. Was the universe trying to tell her that having her outburst wasn't a good thing after all? Even though she felt so light and happy, had she made a catastrophic mistake that necessitated supernatural intervention?

"Don't fear the spirits," Ebenezer hastened to add. "They'll only enhance your life. They'll find meaning you didn't have before, or no longer realized was there."

That struck a chord. Meaning she no longer realized was there.

Her old friend guilt was quick to resurface. She had done something wrong. She'd taken her life for granted and now it was going to take three ghosts to set her straight.

When had she become as bad a person as Ebenezer Scrooge? Did feeling run down, ungenerous, and snappish equate to being as miserable as Scrooge? He wanted orphans and poor people to die. Surely she hadn't become as hopeless as that?

"You can expect the first spirit at midnight. No need to remain awake until then. Trust me, they know how to wake you." He chuckled as if he'd just made a clever joke, but Eliza was too in her head to notice.

When she finally looked up at him again, Ebenezer had already become the static picture of a book cover again and Eliza was alone in the room. She'd known for a while that her life needed to change, but she didn't see how it could. Nothing would change the fact that she was a mother and had to put herself aside often to take care of her kids. They weren't out of the house yet. It was exhausting but that's what she signed up for when she had them. It wouldn't be like that forever, just a phase to get through. And her mother wouldn't magically stop needing help. There was no other family, so Eliza was it. Jacob could manage his schedule and pay better attention to everyone else's activities, but he worked more hours out of the home than Eliza so it made sense that she did more of those things. Plus, she wasn't about to stop the hands of time. She was aging. Her body was preparing for a huge change. She should probably read more about that and book an appointment with her doctor to discuss options, but there wasn't much free time to deal with that and she always managed to put it off again. Would the spirits grant her extra hours and energy to handle everything life threw at her? That's the only solution she could imagine.

She wondered what the spirits could possibly reveal

to her that could ease any of those things, the main sources of her stress.

Who could have foretold that a mundane and unwanted trip to spend Christmas with the in-laws could lead to such an outrageous twist?

❧ 2 ☙
THE GHOST OF CHRISTMAS
PAST

A ny woman of a certain age knows that sleep is a crapshoot. When there's a promise of ghostly visitors, it's a guaranteed failure. Besides, Eliza was known for getting a second wind at about 10:30pm that could keep her going until 2:00 a.m. With ghosts on the way, she didn't bother trying to sleep. She took a Christmas romance novel out of her bag. Even though she'd been sure there wouldn't be an opportunity to rest and read on this trip, she'd packed the book anyway. Turned out to be a wise move. She didn't even notice that midnight had rolled around until the whole bedroom rippled with light. She blinked, wondering if it was her eyes playing tricks on her, then she caught sight of a cream colored shadowy figure near the Scrooge print. Ebenezer was still just a picture, but the figure was undeniably an old-timey looking woman. She was dressed in a flowy but plain dress that was undulating in a breeze Eliza couldn't feel.

The book slipped from Eliza's hands as she stared in

wonder at the being. It was nothing short of amazing. A person could spend their whole life wondering if the afterlife was real. Eliza now had absolute proof. The spirit hadn't spoken a word and Eliza already felt that her life had shifted monumentally.

"Eliza Skragg," the spirit said in a perfectly clear voice. "I didn't know I'd get a chance to meet you like this." The spirit pressed a hand to her eye as if to hold back ethereal tears.

Eliza was taken aback. What was a greeting like that supposed to mean?

"Meet me? Did you know about me before now?"

The spirit nodded. "Of course, dear. Does the name Francis Dixon mean anything to you?"

Eliza silently repeated the name over and over in her head. Francis Dixon. It did ring a bell, but why? Sometimes it took her mind a few minutes to connect the threads of her thoughts. Finally, it clicked into place.

"Francis Dixon!" she exclaimed. "You're my great-grandmother, aren't you?"

The spirit smiled warmly and Eliza felt an unexpected rush of love wash over her.

"Yes indeed, my girl. I've been watching over you since the day you were born."

"Wow! Really?" It was always nice to think that deceased relatives kept a bond with the living but Eliza had wondered if it was just wishful thinking. Not only did she know the afterlife existed, now she knew families did stay connected, even the people you'd never met.

"Yes, really. Now I've been called in to work this extra special project. It's very nice to see and be seen."

"Does that mean you can see everything I do?" The sudden fear that her great-grandmother had seen her in the bathroom, or worse, in the bedroom, made her horribly self-conscious.

"Ah, I'm here to talk about you, dear, and we have a deadline."

That wasn't a reassuring answer, but Eliza bit back all the questions swirling in her mind and remembered that this was like Scrooge's Christmas Eve. Some things would be left unsaid. In this case, perhaps it was better not to know.

"Ok, but I don't know why you're here. I'm not that bad off am I? I thought I was at least a decent person."

Fran laughed gently. "Oh, it's not that you're doing anything wrong, honey. You've just been pulled in so many directions for so long, you've forgotten who you are. I've come to help remind you."

That was vastly more reassuring than assuming she was a selfish miser like Ebenezer Scrooge had been. Although she was quick to remember, he was perfectly lovely to speak with now.

Eliza sighed in relief. "Oh good. I was afraid I'd somehow turned into an awful person when I wasn't paying attention."

"No, no. Don't worry about that, but come on Eliza. There's no time to lose. There's something I need to show you. Take my hand."

Fran floated toward Eliza with her arm outstretched.

Eliza truly felt as perplexed as Ebenezer must have. How was she meant to clasp the hand of a non-physical being?

Fran sensed her confusion.

"Don't think about it. Just do it. Trust me, it all works out."

Fran's presence filled the room with so much peace and love that Eliza did as she was told and reached out for the ghost's hand.

It was not like the Scrooge movies at all. Eliza didn't spring from her bed and jump out a window with Fran. There was no flying through the night. In fact, if asked, Eliza wouldn't say she'd moved at all. It was more like her brain had blacked out for a second and then she came back in a new setting. She wasn't in bed anymore, but she was still in her pajamas and somehow holding hands with a ghost. There was no sensation of Fran's hand in hers. No tingles. No pressure. Nothing. No wonder she'd never been aware of her supernatural presence in Eliza's life. There was no trace.

Slowly, a familiar though long forgotten scene started to form around them, like an old Polaroid picture fading into life.

The walls of a tiny one bedroom apartment appeared around them. The lights were off but the multicolored lights on a three-foot Christmas tree filled the space with a cozy glow. A young couple sat at the bistro table in the dining area. Dining room would be too generous of a word. The entire apartment could be visually sectioned off into two hemispheres. Right through the front door was the no-frills kitchen with the dining area beyond. Looking to the left was the living room. Beyond that the bedroom was on the left hemisphere and the bathroom on the right behind the dining area. That was the entirety of Jacob and Eliza's first apartment together.

The woman was very pregnant and eating home-made Christmas cookies with a mug of hot chocolate. The man was thin and also enjoying a sweet snack. Eliza did a double take.

Who was this gorgeous young man with long wavy hair that fell to his jawline, accentuating a bohemian beard and mustache? Eliza's heart fluttered to see the ghost of Jacob from their early married days. That hair of his was what had drawn her attention to him in the first place. The way it fell over his face when his head bent toward his guitar had made her wild with desire. She'd loved to run her fingers through that hair. It was beachy and effortless for him. He'd wake up in the morning, run his hands through to dislodge the bigger tangles and then it fell into place like a dream. For Eliza to achieve the same look would have taken a professional stylist and at least one hundred dollars.

People joke about "mom haircuts" but it happened to men, too. Jacob had opted for a more professional look by Bella's first birthday and had been clean shaven ever since. Seeing this young Jacob, live and in the flesh again, made Eliza feel like she was watching a movie star. He was so hot!

It was completely bizarre to see her own memory like a play unfolding before her, but this was Jacob and Eliza's third Christmas as a married couple. Bella was only three weeks from making her debut, although neither of them knew that. It was the calm before the storm that was about to sweep them along, relentlessly, for the next seventeen years.

Once she pried her eyes off her young husband, Eliza couldn't get over her own younger self. Even though she was adorably pregnant, she looked like such a lithe young thing. Her skin was firm and radiant, even in the low light. Sleep was getting difficult for her at that stage of pregnancy, but she still looked better rested than modern midlife Eliza had felt in years. She even seemed to have better fashion sense. Late pregnancy made her hot all the time so she was dressed lightly in stretchy pregnancy pajama pants in a darling pink and white checkerboard pattern with a matching pink tank top. Her feet were bare but she'd splurged on a mani/pedi and her nails were a festive Christmas red. She'd read that a pedicure could induce labor, but no such luck. Bella wouldn't come out until she was good and ready. In that regard, some things never changed.

There hadn't been many mani-pedis since then. Who had the luxury of that kind of time? The money was better spent elsewhere anyway. Every time Eliza chose wisely instead of succumbing to a splurge, she would transfer an identical amount of money into either her retirement account or split it between the kids' college funds. Money didn't rain from the sky and she was always mindful of the future. Wouldn't want to get caught short when the time came and the mani/pedi would soon be forgotten.

"Hey," Jacob said softly, the twinkling lights glinting in his eyes. "Can you believe that next Christmas we'll have a daughter to get presents for?"

Eliza smiled and rubbed her belly. Pregnant Eliza was all too aware of the life she'd been carrying in her body for nine months, but she couldn't help but imagine what that first Christmas would be like.

"She'll be almost one by then. What do you think a one-year-old would like for Christmas?"

Jacob's face totally lit up thinking of it.

"I really want to get her a special teddy bear for her first Christmas."

Both past and present Eliza melted at Jacob's earnest declaration. She'd always imagined he was the type of man who would make a great father. She'd been right. He'd also made good on that dream. Bella had received a teddy bear from her father on her first Christmas. She'd named him Nums. Nums was in her bedroom, to this day.

"Aww, honey, that's a great idea." Past Eliza gazed at her husband with pure adoration. The only adoring looks exchanged in her present life were between her and her fluffy West Highland Terrier, Wilkins. She squirmed with the realization that she didn't look at her husband like that anymore. Didn't feel that way about him either. He'd become a constant. A habit. Often an irritant. A companion so well-known as to become almost invisible. If forced to examine the issue, she'd bet Jacob would say the same about her. When had those adoring looks faded away?

"What do you want to get her?" Jacob asked his pregnant bride, leaning forward because he was so eager to hear her answer.

Eliza took a drink of her cocoa and considered the question. She'd had vague fantasies of buying cute little toys and cuddling up together with a stack of picture books, but nothing as specific as a special teddy bear.

"Hmm," she mused. "I'm not sure what exactly I'd like to get her. I do know I want to dress her in one of those little Christmas gowns with tiny patent leather Mary Janes. And a headband with a bow."

Jacob fixed Eliza with an intense stare. "You're going to be the best mom ever. You've been such a trooper this whole pregnancy even though it hasn't been easy. You, and soon this baby, are the most incredible gifts I've ever been given. I just want you to know that."

Eliza moved her hand from her belly and held it out to Jacob, across the table, too choked up to speak.

He quickly took her hand and squeezed, before he stood up.

"Come here. I want to start a new tradition right now. We can call it a practice run before the baby gets here."

Jacob helped her get up from the hard dining chair and led her around the corner to the living room. He settled her on the couch and held up one finger. He scurried to their bedroom and when he came back, he was holding his acoustic guitar. That guitar had featured heavily in their courtship and Eliza never dreamed there would be a future without it.

Somewhere along the line the guitar came out less and less, until it was all but forgotten. Was it still in the back of the closet? Eliza had no idea where it had gone. She hoped he hadn't gotten rid of it when she wasn't looking. Maybe she could get him to play again.

Even though it was playing out before her, Eliza's memory sparked to life. She remembered how she felt when Jacob sat down cross-legged next to their little tree, as he was doing now. She'd thought every

Christmas would be like that forever. Quiet, intimate, just them and the family they were creating. Safe in a little bubble where no one else existed and nothing else mattered. Christmas magic was real then. The work of the holiday was a sacred kind of joy. Making cookies, drinking cocoa together. Singing Christmas carols by the glow of the lights. It wasn't drudgery then. It was new and fresh and something exciting to try. Twenty years later, it was old and tired. The loud expectations of others had come to the forefront. Their own voices were an afterthought, if that. The holidays had become something they owed others, not something they created for themselves. In that sense, maybe she did have more in common with pre-redeemed Scrooge than she thought. It was all a bah humbug she didn't want to cope with. So much work and no reward. Was that just a hazard of growing up? Without Santa Claus and rein-deer to look out for in the frosty night sky, there were no glowing eyes of happy children. Just too cool teens and tired parents desperately trying to find a gift that would recapture some magic for someone, but it didn't work anymore.

Seeing this intimate little Christmas of her past, she longed to have that again. That intimate cocoon of love was its own magic. No presents required.

Was it normal to be envious of your own past self?

Eliza was pulled from her musings when past Jacob settled on the floor and strummed a chord. "This one goes out to my beautiful wife and our daughter-to-be. It's our first Christmas as an almost family of three, so here's a song about another first."

Bathed in only the glow of the Christmas lights, he

started singing "The First Noel." Eliza remembered how nearly every Christmas hymn made her cry that year because the imagery of a mother cradling her infant made her pregnancy hormones go wild. She would soon be a mother cradling an infant. What would her baby look like? How would it feel to see a tiny person that she and Jacob had literally created from nothing? She was on the cusp of creating her own family, with the man she loved, and starting all the traditions they'd carry with them for the rest of their lives. At least, that's what she'd thought.

She watched with her misty eyes as pregnant Eliza quietly sang along with Jacob. It was so beautifully intimate. No one was self-conscious about their voice. Just two people who truly loved each other quietly celebrating a special holiday together. That was something else absent from her present life. When did she and Jacob have any quiet time to just do something like sing together for the sake of it? Even though they had teenagers, their problems were a lot bigger than when they were little. Eliza spent a lot of nights staying up worrying until both kids were snug in bed. There had also been nights when Bella came home in tears because of boy trouble or friend trouble. Sometimes she fought her mother's offers to comfort, but other times she'd cry in her arms like she had as a toddler. With practices and games and all that life entails, they were usually running right up to the moment it was time for bed. At that point, Eliza was ready to pass out. At least until her hormones woke her up again to worry about everything until she either fell asleep again or the alarm went off.

Looking at Past Eliza, she had a tingle of a memory

of how she and Jacob would just curl up together and cuddle because pregnancy had taken a lot of her energy. That was all. No expectation of anything else. Just being there for each other, a couple against the world. It hadn't felt like that for a long time. She'd forgotten it ever had.

Midlife Eliza was moved by the hopeful innocence of that time. Even though she and Jacob had thought they were so mature, they had so much more growing to do. They started to learn fast once Bella came along. There was everything to look forward to then. Things were uncertain now. Where would the kids go to college? Would they go to college? What would they become as they launched their own lives? What would Jacob and Eliza do when it was just the two of them again? Who did she want to be for the second half of her life? It was all difficult to imagine. The excitement level for this next act wasn't nearly as high as it was when Eliza was young. Especially now that her own father was gone. Her future held a lot more endings than beginnings. It wasn't nearly as fun to prepare for all that.

Fran stepped in front of Eliza and the scene started to fade.

"I know we're rushing along here, but time moves fast and there's another important Christmas to revisit."

Eliza nodded. She was already overwhelmed with emotion from the first trip down memory lane.

This time, the room that formed around them was the den of her and Jacob's first house. It was one thing to see herself when she was pregnant, but as she looked around the room, her breath hitched when she saw her parents sitting there. Her father had been gone for eight years now and it was like getting a bonus day to spend with him again. He was sitting on the couch beside his wife, her mother, and both were watching little Bella and Bobby with big smiles and rapt attention. Although she was well aware of the passage of time, Eliza was shocked at the difference in her mother. She looked the part of a grandma in this past version, but the gray hair she had in the past had a lot more white in the present. Her face had many more wrinkles in the present too. Seeing this past version also made it clear how much slower and smaller her mother looked now. She may have enough spirit to drive Eliza up the wall on any given day, but time was coming for her. Even though Eliza always knew it, seeing it made things feel more stark and serious.

It was more bittersweet still to see her dad. His eyes were crinkled with his signature merriment as he watched his grandkids exclaim over the haul around their Christmas tree. Eliza could barely pry her eyes from this living, breathing, version of her dad to the cherubic faces of her kids. She could tell from the packages in front of the kids exactly which Christmas this was. Bella was six and Bobby four. Each had a large wrapped box in front of them. So large, in fact, that Bobby's was about as tall as he was. Bella's was about chest height on her.

"Ok, ok," Jacob laughed. "How about you both open them on the count of three." He was holding up his cell phone to capture the moment on video forever. Although Eliza had seen that video since, it had been focused on the kids, and not the gift givers...her parents. Now that her dad was gone, she desperately wished she had thought to film him while the kids had opened their gifts.

"One...two...three!" Jacob counted and the kids tore into the wrapping paper with gusto.

When they finally got to the presents inside, Bella gasped and clasped her hands to her chest. Her grandfather, handy as he was, had made her a dollhouse.

He'd also made Bobby a garage for his toy cars, complete with fold down ramps so they could be stored in the garage and race too. Bobby jumped up and down and whooped with delight. He wasted no time running to the emptied contents of his stocking and pulling out the new Hot Wheels cars he'd received so he could start playing.

Bella, who shared the sentiment of her little brother, grabbed her new doll and thrust it at Eliza to get it out of the packaging. Gift opening had been halted that morning so they could play with Grandpa's wonderful handmade gifts.

It remained Eliza's favorite Christmas ever.

Unlike on that actual Christmas day, Eliza turned to her father now, tears in her eyes, and watched the look of pride on his face. Her mother looped her arm through his and kissed his shoulder, an expression of congratulations at a job well done.

Eliza had been proud at the time that her parents had been there for the holiday, unlike Jacob's perennially busy parents. Her heart swelled because her dad had made such special gifts with his own hands. She was also proud that her children had appreciated the wonderful gifts. Before she finished freeing the doll from the excessive packaging, she prompted Bella and Bobby with every parent's standard line…"What do you say?"

"Thank you, Grandpa!" both kids exclaimed and then threw themselves into his lap for big hugs and kisses.

The magic of Christmas had been present that year. Eliza and Jacob had invited her parents to spend the day with them, of their own volition. It had been fun to host the holiday, decorate the house, choose the menu, plan activities.

She was on the opposite side of that Christmas now. Currently, the holiday was filled with frustration and fatigue. The joy of childhood was over. Bella wouldn't scream in delight over a new doll anymore. Bobby wouldn't run around the room pumping his little fists in the air because he found two cars in his stocking.

This year, Bella said all she wanted was a new smart phone with a retail price of about a thousand dollars. In lieu of that, she'd take cash. Bobby wanted top of the line gaming headphones and a gaming chair. The prices of both those things had also given Jacob and Eliza sticker shock. Somehow, expensive electronics and cold hard cash didn't create that old fashioned Christmas charm. Seeing that precious little kid Christmas reminded her of that hopeful magic. It did exist in those precious early days. The kids saw wonder in everything and, in turn, Jacob and Eliza had seen it too. It had been everything the media had promised then, because the holiday made her children happy. As stress and responsibility entered Bella and Bobby's lives, the magic faded away for all of them. It must be somewhat inevitable with the passage of time, but Eliza wept for those bygone days as past Eliza had wept for the endless possibilities of her future.

"Our time together is growing short," Fran announced gently.

"Can't I just watch a little longer?" Eliza rasped, voice choked with emotion. Her eyes were still on her dad.

Eliza didn't notice Fran put her arm around her. They stood like that, for another minute only, until the happy sights and sounds from her past faded back into blackness.

Her room at Edward and Dymond's returned around them and Fran went back to her position near the Scrooge picture.

"Thank you for that," Eliza whispered, head in full overload from all she'd just seen. "I'd forgotten some of that."

"It's not all sunshine and roses," Fran said. "The balance of happy and sad, easy and difficult, is what makes a life memorable. Morris and I had our share of arguments and disagreements. It's a very difficult thing for two people to grow in the same direction over the course of a lifetime. There are bound to be divergent paths along the way. Some paths will reconnect, some never will. I just want you to know, you don't ever have to feel trapped."

A fresh batch of tears sprung to Eliza's eyes. Trapped is exactly how she did feel a lot of the time. Trapped by the obligations to her children, husband, mother, job. Her time to unwind and pursue her own interests was always the first thing to be pushed off when someone needed something. She so often found herself thinking, whenever this thing is finally over, I'll be able to do xyz for myself. However, it was more likely that just as whatever "this" was started to wrap up, something else came along that she needed to address and the thing she wanted to do got delayed again, or just plain abandoned. No wonder she felt frustrated and restless. The cycle never ended.

Fran continued. "Every single day is a choice. Remember that. Even if you feel the weight of the world is on you, you can choose to set it down. You don't have to do it all. It isn't possible. It's always a choice. Just like how you and Jacob chose to make singing together a tradition, and how you chose to host the Christmas you wanted. You're the active role in your own story."

"Thank you so much. For everything."

Fran smiled. "You're welcome, dear. Don't be too hard on yourself. Goodness knows everybody else will be. Someone has to be gentle. Might as well be you."

By the time she was done speaking, Fran had faded away into the darkness of night, but her words and the things she'd just shown Eliza echoed through her mind.

Eliza would have dearly loved to talk about more things with Fran, but an hour goes incredibly fast when it's so powerful. There was more work to be done even though her brief visit to the past had ignited her emotions and given her much to ponder. It gave her an all new appreciation for how overwhelmed Scrooge must have felt.

THE GHOST OF CHRISTMAS PRESENT

Brimming with nostalgia, Eliza logged into the photo app on her phone and flipped through early Christmas pictures of her kids. They were so cute and sweet when they were little. Her favorite picture was one of Bobby when he was in second grade and missing his front teeth. It hadn't stopped him from making the biggest smile ever when he opened up a remote controlled dinosaur. He'd been so into dinosaurs then. Jacob and Eliza were half convinced he really would grow up to be a paleontologist. Bella was in the background of the photo, staring down at the half opened package in her lap. Her mouth was hanging open in delighted shock at the American Girl box she'd ripped into. She read every single one of the books, including the classic ones. She'd seemed on her way to developing a lifelong love of history. Both kids had changed dramatically. Bella didn't read anymore, unless it was social media updates and texts. Bobby hadn't mentioned dinosaurs in years.

It wasn't that Eliza didn't love who her children had become, were still becoming. There was no doubt in her mind about how fiercely she loved her children. She worried for them though. Frequently. She didn't know what the future held for them. The world seemed a lot darker and scarier than it had when she was a teenager and kids weren't as sheltered as she'd been. How could they be? Everything was on the internet, whether you went looking for it or not. Wars, climate change, mass shootings, natural disasters, racism, sexism, pandemics, human trafficking. Name your worst nightmare and it was right there, happening in real life, in the newsfeed of any app.

Eliza shivered as she contemplated the difference between the innocent children in her old family photos and the world-weary teenagers of now.

Maybe that wasn't the only reason she shivered. Her body may have registered the shift in energy that her mind wasn't paying attention to.

"I am the ghost of Christmas Present," a thin voice announced. This spirit did not have the presence Francis Dixson had. In fact, Eliza had a difficult time even locating this one. Bathed in the glow of her phone, she squinted into the darkness looking for a ghostly glimmer she didn't find.

"Are you still here?" she asked.

"I am. Sorry, let me turn up the brightness a bit."

Once again, Eliza's gaze fell to the wall with the Scrooge picture. Eventually, she saw what looked like a vertical ribbon with a dull grayish hue.

"Is that you? I'm sorry, you don't look like what I was expecting."

"It's because I'm present. I haven't happened yet and I'm not going to be. I'm just now. Always."

It wasn't the sort of answer Eliza could really wrap her mind around but it sort of made sense. In a really weird way.

"You're not human?"

"I'm a spirit."

"Forgive me for asking, but the spirit of what?"

"The present. I said that straightaway."

Eliza quickly realized that this was going to be a very different experience than she'd just had. The Scrooge movies hadn't prepared her for this at all.

"You did. Yes. Sorry. I just..." She wasn't sure how to complete that thought, and it wasn't because brain fog had stolen her words.

"I know. Humans. Limited perception capabilities, but you will do very well with what I need to share with you. Close your eyes."

So everything was going to be different from Fran's visit. This night was definitely going to keep her on her toes.

Eliza closed her eyes, completely unsure what to expect.

A scene didn't fade into view, but she began to hear voices. Familiar voices. Dymond and Edward. Eliza's heart sank. The last thing she wanted was to deal with those two anymore than she absolutely had to. She had no idea what good could possibly come from this.

Dymond was speaking first.

"I don't know why you even said that. You didn't have to be such a dick. They'd only just gotten here for goodness' sake."

"It was a joke! I didn't know she wouldn't be able to take a joke. She was way out of line."

"You only attacked her marriage in front of her husband and kids. What did you think she'd do?"

"Uh...laugh. Like a normal person. Not start screaming like a psycho."

Eliza bristled. They were talking about her and her outburst. Uncharacteristically, she still didn't feel bad about it. She'd been pushed far enough and there was no reason Edward should have said what he did. She only stood up for herself, in a loud, dramatic manner, but that was what she needed to do. She was curious what they'd say next.

"She wasn't a psycho. She had a point."

"A point!" Edward scoffed.

"Yes," Dymond's voice sounded a little wobbly.

"Oh God. Now you're going to start crying? Is it national overreact if you're a woman day?"

"No, she had a point about you, Edward. Are you thinking about cheating all the time? Why would you even say that to her? It doesn't even make sense."

"I told you, it was a joke. Geez. You're not very fun anymore. Maybe I should have asked you if you're the one cheating."

Eliza had never been a big fan of Dymond, but she hadn't been openly rude to her. Not until her little outburst anyway. It could have had a gentler delivery, but she really had been upset about Derby clocking her son without so much as a "No, no. We don't hit our cousins with toys, sweetheart." She was tired of biting her tongue and watching Derby run wild without any input from his parents. Edward should definitely have known better. He and Michelle had three kids of their own. Come to think of it, Michelle had always been the one doing the parenting when Eliza was around. Dymond was doing this for the first time and there wasn't a rule book. Suddenly, Eliza felt compelled to cut her some slack.

"Why are you being so mean?" Dymond couldn't hide that she was crying. She wasn't full on sobbing yet, but her voice hitched in that familiar way.

"I'm not mean. I'm just mad because Jacob's hysterical wife threw a hissy fit for no reason. I never did understand what he sees in her."

"Spoiler alert, there's nothing to see in you either," Eliza muttered, but neither Edward nor Dymond could hear her.

"She was right, Edward. You should have apologized to her and Jacob for saying that. She was right about Derby too. I was totally zoned out. He shouldn't be attacking his cousins like that."

Eliza could have been knocked over with a feather. She had no idea why Dymond was defending her. She didn't think Dymond thought of her at all, but here she was, on her side.

"Attacking? He's three. They're teenagers. What's he going to do, hurt their widdle fweelings? If they can't stand up to a three year old, they aren't going to make it in this world."

Eliza's blood was starting to boil all over again.

"I saw Bobby's knee in the kitchen. He rolled up his pant leg and he had a big purple bump. That was Derby's fault. I made him look at it and tell Bobby he was sorry. He's never going to get accepted to preschool if he thinks it's okay to hurt people."

"He's never going to go to preschool if he doesn't learn to use the toilet either and that's been looking pretty hopeless."

Dymond exhaled a ragged sigh.

The voices were silent for long enough that Eliza began to wonder whether this visit was over, but then Dymond spoke again in a very small voice.

"You knew I wanted to host Christmas because I wanted to get to know Jacob and Eliza better. You knew I really want her to like me. Right now, it sort of feels like you acted that way to make sure she never would."

This was news to Eliza. The two women couldn't even have a surface level conversation. Dymond never asked her any questions. From her perspective, Dymond couldn't have cared less about her. How could their interactions have been so twisted around that neither one thought they could get through to each other? Or were they both so distracted and ground down by life that they couldn't connect anymore? Although at very different life phases, maybe she had more in common with Dymond than she'd thought.

There was no reason to lie. Dymond didn't know Eliza could hear this conversation. She was obviously speaking from her heart, only Edward refused to hear her.

Edward scoffed. "Who cares if Eliza likes you? Her opinion doesn't mean anything."

"It matters to me. You knew that. She's as close as I'll ever get to having a sister. I always wished for a sister."

"Some sister. She's old enough to be your mother. Anyway, I'm sick of talking about her. It sounds like Derby's jumping up and down in his crib. Why don't you think about dealing with that?"

Dymond took a hiccupy breath.

"Maybe I never should have married you." Her voice was very quiet but it had the dawning of power in it. Eliza recognized that tone. Although she'd been much louder about it earlier, it was the same note of sudden self-assurance and self-worth.

Eliza never dreamed that Edward would treat his trophy wife– No. That wasn't fair to Dymond, whom she was finally seeing as a person instead of a caricature. She never dreamed he would treat his wife so poorly.

"Maybe *I* shouldn't have gotten married again. Should have learned my lesson the first time. It sucks."

The voices started to sound farther and farther away until Eliza couldn't pick up what they were saying.

"Wow," she said to her odd, thin, spirit. "I wasn't expecting that."

"I'm not sure what it was. I'm only here now."

This was the strangest interaction Eliza had ever had with a...person? That wasn't right, but would have to do.

"Ok, well, I appreciate you letting me listen in on that. I haven't been fair to Dymond. I still don't really know her, but I know something she's dealing with. That paints her in a whole different light."

"I'm glad this was insightful for you, but we aren't through yet."

"Oh! Sorry. I thought they were done talking."

"They are. We have a new pair to visit now. Listen."

Eliza closed her eyes again, even though there wasn't much to see in the dark anyway. Once again, she was surprised by what she heard.

The first sound was a knock on a door. Well, presumably a door. What else would be knocked on?

Then a pause of silence, and a furtive whisper.

"Bella, are you up? Can I come in?"

Bobby! What was he doing knocking on his sister's door at this hour?

"Yeah," Bella's groggy voice answered.

Eliza heard a door open and close and tried to brace herself for whatever two teenagers would talk about in the middle of the night.

"You can't sleep either?" Bobby asked.

"No. It smells weird in here. Like synthetic pine trees. It's giving me a headache."

"Yeah. My room smells like gingerbread and it's either making me hungry or sick. I can't tell which."

"How's your knee? Does it still hurt?"

Eliza's heart melted. There wasn't so much as a trace of snark in Bella's voice. She sounded genuinely concerned for her brother.

"A little, but that's because I drifted off and I was pressing it into the mattress and it started hurting."

"That sucks. That kid is a menace. I can't wait to get out of here."

"Me neither. Edward and his new family are so cringe."

"Especially Uncle Edward. He's toxic AF. Mom was pretty awesome though. I wish I could bitch everyone out and stomp off like that."

"You do that at home all the time."

Eliza could practically hear Bella's eyes roll.

"Shut up. I don't do it all the time, but Mom never does it. She stood up to toxic masculinity in our own family. On Christmas Eve! I wish I would have recorded it. Mom would go viral for sure."

Eliza could hardly believe what she was hearing. Bella seemed in awe of her mother for a change, and dare she think it, proud?

"Yeah, that was pretty badass. The only thing that would have made it better is if she'd hit Uncle Edward, or smashed her glass on the floor."

"Yeah. Or thrown it in his face. He was being such a fucker."

Eliza's first instinct was to bristle at the language. How could her little angels be using such coarse language, but then she remembered what she was like as a teen and relaxed. They were talking to each other privately after all.

"This is the worst Christmas Eve we ever had." Bobby sounded introspective, but also his words were tinged with a sadness that wrenched Eliza's heart.

"Yeah, Mom didn't even get to make us watch *A Christmas Carol*."

"I like watching *A Christmas Carol*. It doesn't really feel like Christmas without that."

"Mom didn't tuck us in either. That kinda sucks."

Eliza put her hand to her chest, as if she could press this sincere declaration from her teenagers into her heart forever. She did make it a point to tuck her kids in on Christmas Eve, even though they weren't little anymore. It made her feel good, but she hadn't realized that Bella and Bobby enjoyed it too. They never let on, being irascible teenagers and all.

"I hope she doesn't stay in her room all day tomorrow. Mom knows how to make Christmas fun. Like how she makes us hot chocolate and lets us eat cookies for breakfast on Christmas day."

Bella laughed. "I like that too. I can't imagine Aunt Dymond will do that. She'll probably have some weird whole grain spread that looks pretty on the Gram. It'll taste like dirt and we'll have to choke it down and pretend it's delicious."

Bobby made a fake retching noise and they both laughed. "Maybe we could pull a Mom and flip over some platters of food and then storm back to our rooms. That would be fun."

"It would be, but I'd still rather have Mom's Christmas breakfast."

"Me too." Bobby sighed and both kids were silent for a few beats.

Eliza thought this visit had ended until she heard Bobby speak up again, quietly.

"Bella?"

"What?"

"If you're not too sleepy, we could watch *A Christmas Carol* on YouTube. Is your phone charged?"

"My phone's always charged. I don't let the battery run down like you do."

"Ok, so which version do you want to watch?"

"Climb in and let's pick one out."

Eliza heard the rustling of blankets as she imagined her kids nestling into bed together as they had when they were little.

Their voices faded away as they started to discuss their favorite film versions of the story and Eliza's heart filled nearly to bursting. Even better than a family viewing. Eliza was overcome with love imagining Bella and Bobby carrying on that little tradition together. It was a simple thing, but she saw that it had made an impact on them. Just like the cocoa and cookie breakfasts. She'd started that when they were little and woke up at 4:00 a.m. to open presents. It was a practical thing then. She and Jacob hadn't been able to put out presents until they were sure both kids were asleep, which was usually after midnight. By the time they got to bed, they were exhausted, but the kids were up and at 'em just a few hours later. The last thing she wanted to do at 4:00 a.m. was make breakfast, so cocoa and cookies it was.

Her reverie about the origins of Christmas cookie breakfast faded when she became aware of a new sound. A very familiar sound. Jacob's gentle snoring filled her ears as if she was lying right next to him.

"Are you kidding me?" Eliza asked the room, the spirit, no one in particular. "After all that drama, he's just peacefully snoozing away? Getting a good night's rest while I'm over here literally analyzing my entire life with paranormal visitors?"

The thought made her magma rise, replacing the warmth she felt from her kids with the heat of anger. She couldn't be sure if it was perimenopausal rage, something that seemed to be happening more and more, or if it was just regular rage. Whichever it might be, she didn't care. She felt it and it wouldn't be ignored.

Even if she wasn't being visited by spirits, she would

not have been sleeping. Her brain would be playing a loop of all the irritating things that had happened to her that day. From the neediness of her mom, to Jacob's stupid joy about visiting these people, to the kids being tethered to their devices.

She soaked in the feeling of vindication that she'd been right about visiting Edward and Dymond. How had she known that something awful would happen and Jacob was so ignorantly unaware? She'd only been dealing with Edward since she and Jacob began dating. Jacob had known Edward from the moment he was born. He was a jerk, plain and simple. He'd been that way since she met him. Why couldn't Jacob grow up and see things for what they were? No. Instead he just snored away in a guest bed without a care in the world, while his wife was up agonizing about everything just a few feet away. It made her want to scream.

Before she could wake up the house with her howling anger, the snoring faded away and her bizarre friend brightened up a bit near the Scrooge picture.

"There is just one more scene we have to visit and then our time together will come to an end."

"Lead on," Eliza said, trying to get her head around everything she was hearing.

This time, the sound turned up slowly, like they were stumbling across a radio program already in progress.

Her mother's voice was soft and low with sleepiness, but she'd know that voice anywhere.

"—can you believe it, Harold? Eliza let Jacob haul them all off to his stupid brother's house and left me here all alone for Christmas. It just isn't right. If you were still here, you wouldn't have stood for it. I guess the kids just don't understand that I'm not going to be around forever."

Eliza felt the tension in her chest tighten. Really? Even in her late night musings to her dead husband, she couldn't acknowledge that Eliza had so many different directions she had to go in? Of course she knew her mother wasn't going to live forever. She thought about that all the time, but it didn't mean she had to be at her mother's beck and call every day. Jacob's family wasn't immortal either. No matter what you did in life, there would come a day when you ran out of time with everyone. There would always be regrets, but everything was a juggling act. Nothing was a guarantee and Eliza could only do the best she could with the time she had each day. It was impossible to make everyone happy.

Eliza's mother sighed.

"Well, if you were still here, I wouldn't be alone in the first place. Ah, Harold. I miss you. You know that? As irritating as you could be, I sure do miss you being here."

That was a sentiment Eliza could sympathize with. She missed her father too. Every time the kids reached a new milestone and their grandfather wasn't there to see it, Eliza felt an ache in her heart. She knew it was different for her mother, rattling around in that house of memories all by herself. She imagined what her mother must look like at the moment. Maybe she was lying in bed, talking to the empty side where her dad used to lie. Maybe she was sitting in her living room chair, with her afghan over her lap, talking to the picture of Harold she kept on the end table.

As frustrated as Eliza could get with her mother, it did break her heart to think of an old woman alone on Christmas Eve. Even if they had already done all the traditional Christmas things with her, including dinner and gifts.

"Oh well," Eliza's mother continued. "I guess the silver lining is I can do whatever I want for a change."

Eliza's mother chuckled quietly. "Maybe I'll turn my Nat King Cole Christmas album all the way up and dance around the living room in my robe and pajamas."

Eliza brightened at the thought.

"Yes!" she whispered, even though there was no one to hear her, except maybe the weird spirit. "There have to be some perks to being alone. Absolutely do whatever you want!"

"And maybe I'll get out one place setting of Mom's old Christmas china and serve my Lean Cuisine on it."

Eliza's mother actually giggled, clearly tickled by the idea of a mass produced frozen entree being served on fine china.

"I could call Josie and Judy."

Eliza's aunts Josie and Judy were both younger than her mother, Jillian, and she'd often thought they should do more together than they did. Calling them for Christmas was a great idea.

"If the weather holds, I might even go to see a movie at the theater. Wouldn't that be a treat?"

The more she talked, the more excited she sounded and the calmer Eliza felt. It wasn't the end of the world to pull back a little. At least now and then anyway. She was lucky her mother had enough health and mental capacity that she could still do things independently.

Just because she preferred not to didn't mean it was imperative Eliza had to step in. Her mother would probably never admit it, but this secret insight was very enlightening, and positive.

The list of ideas quelled until there was no more sound other than Eliza exhaling a big breath of relief.

"My journey with you is complete. Good luck. I hope everything turns out well."

"Thank you." Eliza didn't know what else to say as her very unusual guide quickly faded into nothingness.

Strange as the ghost of Christmas Present was, her head spun with all she'd just witnessed. Opposite emotions flooded through her, anger and sadness at the exchange between Edward and Dymond, but peace and hope at the evidence of a solid bond between Bella and Bobby. Then back to anger at Jacob's oblivion, but a sense of relief that her mother could step up for herself after all.

As she tried to process these new depths of information she'd just gleaned, the room grew darker in a way that indicated something else otherworldly was going on.

❧ 4 ❧
THE GHOST OF CHRISTMAS
FUTURE

The spirits were getting increasingly darker. Not necessarily in their messages, but physically. Or maybe metaphysically was a better word for it. The future was even stranger than the present, and murkier.

The Ghost of Christmas Future made the 2:00 a.m. room look brighter by managing to be darker than the night air around it. If pressed to describe it at all, the best Eliza could say was a black hole. It was just an impossibly black sphere, which was also hovering near the Scrooge print. That must have been the source powering this whole incredible night. Everything seemed to start with that.

Next, she couldn't help but think of Tiny Tim.

"I don't want to see anything about dying," Eliza said. "No matter who it is. That's something we all have to face eventually, I'm well aware of that and I don't want to pretend deal with it before I have to do it for real. Can we agree on that?"

"This is not a message of death, but of life. A possibility, and nothing more."

The future was definitely weirder than the present. It had an audible voice, but it was all over the place. Almost like a different person was speaking each word.

"Are you..." Eliza struggled for the words to pin down what she wanted to ask. "Just one being or many?"

"I'm a state of flux. The future is never truly known. Every thought, every action can change the outcome. I am a combination of possibilities based on the trajectory your life has taken so far. I am also partly made up of your wishes and desires. What you are and what you could be."

Fran and the Present had already done an impeccable job of blowing her mind. Wrapping her mind around what the Future had just said was futile.

"Are you saying this vision is nothing more than a dream?"

"It is one of many possible realities you could live. A dream is never real. This vision is wholly possible."

Again, not an answer she could totally grasp, but it sounded more substantial than a dream.

"Ok," Eliza said. "Lead on."

She did not expect what started to happen.

The other two spirits had eased her into the transition subtly. The future was not subtle. It was more like every sci-fi movie she'd ever watched, when a spaceship jumps into warp speed, or hyperdrive, or whichever terminology they use. Countless tiny pinpricks of light filled the room, like she was floating amidst a tightly condensed night sky of stars. One of them started glowing brighter and looming larger until she felt a sensation of rushing toward it. The other points of light streaked by like long lines. Just as she thought she would fall down from dizziness, everything was still, and then the normal world blinked to life around her.

She was in her own home, although it was slightly different than when she'd left it. The kids' backpacks were nowhere in sight. Neither were any of the little things they managed to keep strewn around no matter what.

Some Christmas decorations were up, but not all of them. Not most of them. The only stockings hung on the mantle belonged to her and Jacob. There was no sign of Bella or Bobby's stockings. The tree was up but it only had a fraction of the ornaments they usually put on it. They were spaced out, leaving the bulk of the bedazzling to the tinsel and lights. The star wasn't even on top.

As she wondered what kind of future would leave her bereft of any trace of her children, she startled when she saw the figures of her and Jacob sitting at the dining room table. She glided closer to get a better view.

First, she noticed that Jacob's hair was a little thinner and grayer than it currently was. His physique was also a bit softer.

Eliza steeled herself to gaze upon her future self, but she jumped back when she saw. Instead of an older version of her own face, it was as if someone had put a blur filter over her. She couldn't get a clear picture of the woman, although she knew without a doubt it was herself.

These future iterations of her and Jacob were finishing their Christmas dinner. The table was only set for the two of them and it didn't even have its customary holiday tablecloth.

Whenever in time this might be, clearly it was after the kids had grown and gone. She was looking at the empty nester versions of her and Jacob. It was a time she tried not to imagine because she had no idea how it would look. Their lives had been so centered on the kids, they were out of practice being a couple. She'd heard stories of older couples finding they'd grown in opposite directions and wanting to pursue new things... separately. The idea sounded both terrifying and exhilarating in equal measures. Judging from what she could see in this under-decorated future, things weren't looking so vibrant and dynamic for this version of Eliza and Jacob.

The dinner spread, for instance, made her sad. It looked like no one had been interested in cooking anything. There was a run of the mill dinner sausage, boxed mac and cheese, and a bowl of green beans. The beans were clearly from the freezer section of the grocery store.

This was the type of meal Eliza would make for her kids on busy school nights when everyone was rushing home from work and school and had some other event to be at in an hour or less. It wasn't the type of fare she'd ever served for a holiday.

Jacob finished his last bite of sausage, chewed momentarily, and then stood up to clear his dishes. Eliza didn't even bother to look up. Although her face wasn't clear, Eliza could tell that Future Eliza's head was angled toward the windows, her mind presumably lost in thought.

When Jacob came back from the kitchen, he brought a small gift bag with him. He carried it over to Eliza and set it down beside her. She pushed her plate out of the way and stood.

"Oh," Future Eliza said in a dull tone. "Let me grab your gift and we can open them together."

She took her dishes away and disappeared to get the gift.

Present Eliza was shocked. They'd never opened gifts at the table before. They always opened them near the Christmas tree. Even before the kids. What were the future versions of them doing?

When Eliza came back, she was holding a small wrapped box.

"Merry Christmas," they mumbled to each other and then set about slowly unwrapping their gifts.

Eliza was quicker, since she only had to reach into the bag and pull her gift out from the tissue paper. She found herself holding a small gift pack of shower gel and body lotion from Bath & Body Works. The scent was nothing special, just a generic vanilla. She usually chose floral scents for herself. After all the years, didn't Jacob know what kind of scents she preferred? Not that she was averse to vanilla, it was perfectly fine, but the effort seemed so minimal. So impersonal. She was hurt, on behalf of her potential future self.

"How nice. Thank you." Future Eliza said the words pleasantly enough, but there was an undercurrent of disappointment, although Jacob probably wouldn't notice that.

"You're welcome," he said, and then finished unwrapping his gift. As the paper fell away, it revealed a mug with a photo of a tropical beach and the words "Key Largo" in a fancy orange script.

"Does this mean we're finally going to go?" asked Jacob with a quiver of cautious excitement in his voice.

"Go?" Future Eliza cocked her head.

"Yeah," Jacob said, finally getting some enthusiasm into his voice. "Why don't we take that trip to the Keys? We've been thinking about it for years. The kids are gone now, we don't have to worry about school schedules. We both have vacation time available. Let's finally plan it. Just us."

Although Present Eliza hadn't had the same passion for the potential trip to the Keys as Jacob, she certainly wasn't opposed to it. As far as reconnecting went, that sounded like a fun way to do it. Trying something new together. Making new memories. She found herself holding her breath in anticipation of what her future self would say.

"It's a nice idea," she said, "But the kids' college expenses haven't gone away and we promised to do our best not to saddle them with debt for the rest of their lives. Plus, we're going through Mom's savings like crazy just so she can be taken care of well. If she outlives the money, we either have to move her to a low quality facility that insurance would pay for, or use our own savings to keep her where she is. I don't think a trip is the most responsible use of our money right now. There's too many unknowns."

Jacob nodded and frowned at the scene on his mug.

"Of course," he said in a quiet voice, all the enthusiasm long gone again. "There's always something more important to save for. But thanks for the nice mug. I'll pretend I'm on the beach when I drink from it."

"That's what I thought you'd do," Future Eliza stammered. "Since we can't go yet, at least it's a nice piece of the Keys you can have for now. We'll get there one day."

"Yeah, I know," Jacob said. "I appreciate it."

Their words sounded hollow even to Present Eliza. Was that really what she sounded like when she discussed finances with Jacob? Although the threat of the huge expense of nursing facilities was already in one of the worry tabs of Eliza's mind, seeing how deflated and bland she and Jacob were in this future made her worry even more.

Eliza keenly felt that all her responsibilities were tearing them apart. Disconnecting them bit by bit, but surely this isn't how her life would be? They were acting like joyless strangers in their own home. On Christmas of all days!

"You're welcome," Future Eliza said glumly.

After a pause, with both looking wistfully at their lackluster Christmas gifts, Jacob spoke up again.

"Should we call the kids now?"

Future Eliza held up her wrist to check her watch before nodding.

"Yeah, we can see what they're up to."

Jacob pulled out his phone, put it on speaker, and dialed.

The phone rang a few times before someone picked up and a lot of background noise came through before Bella's voice finally said, "Hello!"

"Hi honey, Merry Christmas!" Jacob said. "Sounds pretty busy there. What are you up to?"

"We're waiting in line to get into the theater," Bella replied. Now that she said it, the background noises made sense.

Was Bella off on a trip during the holiday like Jacob's parents always took?

"Oh! I didn't know you were doing that. What are you going to see?" Eliza asked.

"Kendra knows a guy who got us last minute discount tickets so we're seeing the new Broadway production of *A Christmas Carol*! Ryan Reynolds is playing Scrooge!"

That was unexpected in many ways. The name Kendra wasn't familiar, so maybe it was a friend Bella was going to meet in college or at work? She didn't know how many months or years in the future this vision was, but Ryan Reynolds as Scrooge was also a surprise, although she was sure he'd do a great job in the role.

"That's amazing!" Eliza exclaimed. "Sounds like you're having the time of your life."

"It's been great," Bella agreed. "Plus, I might not be watching a new movie version, but I thought you'd appreciate me seeing a live production instead."

Jacob chuckled. "Yes, that's really cool, honey. We'll be watching the movie tonight, but I think your show will be a lot more exciting."

"You'll have to tell us all about it later," Eliza added.

"I will," Bella promised. "Ok, we're getting close to the front of the line now. I gotta go. Talk to you later. Love you!"

"Love you too," Jacob and Eliza both said and then the call disconnected.

After the call, Jacob had a little more sparkle in his eyes. It was a marked difference from the dull look he'd had when he was finishing dinner with only his wife.

"Sounds like she's having a magical holiday adventure, huh? Who'd have thought our girl would be taking in a Broadway show for Christmas." He turned to Future Eliza with the first hint of happiness on his face.

"Yes. I'm glad she's having such a good time. What an experience! Broadway at Christmas."

They sat in wistful silence for a few beats before Jacob turned back to the phone.

"Well, is Bobby up by now, do you think?"

Future Eliza nodded.

"He's six hours ahead of us. Should be after dinner for him."

"Right. I don't know why I always think they're behind us."

Present Eliza was surprised. Clearly, Bobby was off in the world somewhere in a different time zone. So both of her children were traveling. Sounded like they were doing well, whatever they were up to. A piece of her brain that was relegated to worrying about the kids relaxed a little.

"Ok," said Jacob. "Then let's see how his day went." He pressed the button to connect with Bobby and the phone rang a few times. Just before Eliza thought it would go to voicemail, Bobby picked up.

"Joyeux Noël maman et papa!"

It was clearly Bobby's voice, but Eliza had never heard him speak French before. She knew he planned to take French as his foreign language credit for junior and senior year of high school, but he wasn't there yet. Future Bobby's accent sounded pretty good to her. Apparently, it was going to work out well for him.

"Don't 'papa' me," Jacob joked. "Makes me sound like an old man."

Bobby laughed. "You are an old man, dad."

"Getting there," Jacob agreed, "But I've got some time left."

"Merry Christmas, honey!" Eliza said. "Did you have a good day?"

"Bien sûr. We just finished dinner a little bit ago and it was delicious. I may never need to eat again."

"Ooh, what did you have?" Jacob sounded genuinely excited now. No surprise since Eliza had seen the sad meal he'd just finished.

"Foie gras, turkey, bread and cheese, frisée salad, green beans. My favorite part was the dessert. Madame Laurent made a traditional Bûche de Noël."

"Oh," exclaimed Eliza. "I've seen those on the baking show I like to watch. They can be really pretty, too."

"It was. I'll have to text you guys some pictures before I go to bed."

"What are you up to now?" Jacob asked.

"Mostly digesting," Bobby answered. "But playing some games too."

"Well, we'll let you get back to it," Eliza said. "Glad everything's going so well."

"Thanks. It's amazing."

"We love you!" Eliza and Jacob said at the same time.

"Love you too. Talk soon."

The call disconnected and Jacob and Eliza fell into silence again. Jacob tucked the phone back into his pocket and looked around the room aimlessly.

Eliza absently opened up her vanilla lotion, squirted a dollop onto the back of her hand, and rubbed it in.

"Smells nice," she said quietly.

"Glad you like it," Jacob said. He stood, new mug in hand. "I'm going to wash this out and get a cup of coffee. You want anything?"

"No, I'm good."

Jacob disappeared into the kitchen and Eliza just sat at the table, staring at her gift in silence.

"El!" Jacob called from the kitchen. "You wanna watch *Die Hard*?"

He had to be teasing.

"Don't you want to watch *A Christmas Carol* with me?"

"Haven't we watched every version of that in existence by now?" Jacob called back.

"But that's our thing. Even Bella's going to watch the show. If we put it on now, it'll be like we're watching it right along with her."

"I suppose," Jacob replied, but it didn't sound very convincing.

Present Eliza stared in shock at the bland, overly polite Christmas before her. That was nothing like what she dreamed Christmas should be. None of it was right —the meal, the gifts, the atmosphere, her and Jacob. She knew it would probably be weird to transition to being just the two of them again, but she didn't think it would turn out that painfully. The only animation between Jacob and Eliza had been when they spoke to the kids.

She might not be able to see Future Eliza's face, but that was a sad, unfulfilled shell of a woman. She didn't need to see faces to know that.

Jacob had no spark either, and she didn't like to see him like that. She thought the stress of raising teenagers balanced with the needs of her aging mother would relent sometime. That mythical day, she expected they'd sigh in relief, shake off their run-down selves, and set about the work of reconnecting, recharging, and reimagining what their lives would be. It hadn't occurred to her that they'd be too far gone, irreparably changed, to course correct. The thought was both sobering and scary.

Thankfully, the scene began to warp away in the same manner it had appeared. Her bizarre black hole guide was nowhere that she could perceive, but the pinpricks of light and movement lines came back. Once again, just as she was starting to feel dizzy, it all slowed and a new scene sprang to life around her.

This place was the exact opposite of the future she'd just left.

The setting was unfamiliar but instantly warm and comforting. It was a small dining room but light, bright, and packed with smiling people.

Again, Future Eliza's face was a blur, but the rest of the people were clear and totally unknown.

Future Eliza stood at the head of the small square table with a platter of turkey in her hands. She was setting it on the table to the celebratory whoops of the people around her. To her left sat an elderly man with a few wisps of white hair on his bald pate. He was wearing a gaudy Christmas sweater, and Present Eliza quickly realized they all wore different hideous sweaters. His had a cartoonish moose head complete with blinking lights hanging in its felt antlers.

Across from him, a wavy-haired redhead sat in a powerchair. She was definitely younger than the man. Somewhere comfortably in middle age though. Present Eliza admired her gorgeous hair, even though her outfit did little to complement it. Her sweater looked like it was made out of red faux fur, like a Muppet, with appliquéd sequin candy canes all over.

Finally, across from Eliza sat a man with cropped black hair, navy blue glasses, and light brown skin. His sweater may have been the worst of all. It was a collage of reindeer faces. Some from actual pictures of reindeer, others of cartoon reindeer. It was so busy, Eliza thought her eyes might go crossed from looking at it.

"I didn't think you were really going to make a turkey!" the red-haired woman exclaimed boisterously. "This was supposed to be an easy, no stress celebration!"

"Leave it to our sweet Eliza to put us to shame," the older man joked with a twinkle in his eye.

"It smells delicious," the other man offered.

"Thank you, Steven," Future Eliza said. "We just like to pick on each other. It's all in good fun. Besides, you all made things too."

"Not me!" said the older man gesturing to the dish of canned cranberry sauce and the bag of dinner rolls next to it.

"Stop it, Richard," Eliza admonished in a jokey tone. "You made a pumpkin pie too!"

"So what?" Richard asked. "I just used a refrigerated pie crust and dumped a can of pumpkin puree inside. It may not even be edible."

"Lord," the redhead put her head in her hands. "I hope you put some spice in the puree before you baked it."

"Ha ha. Very fun, Ginny. I'm old but I'm not stupid." He pulled a silly face before adding, "Well, shit. *Did* I remember to put the spice in? Now you've got me wondering."

Steven looked as though he didn't know whether to laugh or be concerned. Judging from Eliza's comment, he seemed to be new to the group.

"What did you bring?" Ginny asked the bespectacled man.

"I made an approximation of my grandmother's sweet potato casserole. I think she had a secret ingredient she never told any of us about, because it never tastes exactly like hers."

"Well, it smells delicious and sweet potatoes are my favorite," Eliza said.

Steven appeared to catch Eliza's eye and smile. "Then I'm really glad I brought them."

Eliza thought she detected a faint blush start to creep into Future Eliza's cheeks, even though the details of her face were a blur. She understood why. Steven was an attractive man, and glancing at Future Eliza's hands, there were no rings on her fingers. It didn't necessarily mean anything, as Eliza didn't like to cook or clean with her rings on, but this collection of unknown people coming together for a holiday meal gave Eliza plenty to ponder.

"I brought the green bean casserole," Ginny announced with pride.

"Ah," interjected Richard, "But did you use fresh beans or canned?"

"Canned, of course. What do you take me for?"

The old man's eyes twinkled and he nodded in approval.

"Atta girl! Didn't think you'd try to put any of us to shame, but had to check."

Future Eliza glanced around the table, no doubt running through a mental checklist to account for everything. "Is there anything I've forgotten?"

"Butter?" Steven reminded gently.

"For Richard's rolls! Yes!" Eliza hurried off to fetch the butter.

"They aren't only my rolls," Richard called after her. "I'm willing to share, you know."

"You know what I mean!" Eliza called back from the kitchen.

Present Eliza gazed at the faces of those gathered around the table. How in the world would a future version of herself meet people like this? She'd lamented the absence of close friends in her life. Although she was loosely in touch with her best friends from high school, it wasn't like the movies. None of them were independently wealthy. None of them had inherited a beach house on Martha's Vineyard. They didn't drop everything in their lives to summer together every year. At best, they had access to each other's social media accounts and wished each other happy birthday or offered holiday greetings. Present Eliza wished very much she had a close girlfriend she could go to coffee with and have a little fun. Just watching Ginny sit at the table and trade quips and jabs with the group filled Eliza with longing.

In this strange future, she apparently had such a girl-friend and two good male friends as well. It wasn't a vision of Christmas she'd ever imagined, but it felt homey and fun. As charming as a movie but better, because it was this Eliza's real life.

Future Eliza hurried back and set the butter on the table.

"Ok," she said, glancing around the tabletop once more. "I think that's everything. Shall we have a toast before we dig in?"

Richard rolled his eyes in an exaggerated way for comedic effect. "I'm starving, woman! Can't we get on with it?"

Eliza put her hands on her hips and tilted her head toward Richard.

"You'll survive," she said.

He winked and raised his water glass.

Eliza remained standing at the head of the table and everyone held up the glass of whatever they were drinking. She took a brief moment to look at each of the guests gathered and then began.

"I used to dread the holiday season. It was so full of obligation and expectation. I felt smothered and stressed about the whole thing. Now, thanks to you all, I can honestly say I'm happy to be here. To have good food, with good friends." She nodded toward Steven, "And new friends. I hope this isn't the beginning of a tradition that will ever feel obligatory, but a gathering we'll look forward to for many years to come."

"Here, here!" Ginny exclaimed. They all clinked glasses, took a sip, and Eliza sat down.

"But that's not all!" Ginny said as Richard reached for the steaming casserole next to him.

Ginny raised her glass. "I'd also like to offer a toast."

Richard groaned but folded his hands in his lap rather than scooping out the food he'd been going for.

Everyone swiftly lifted their glasses again.

"It's been a rough go for me lately." She gestured her free hand to her wheelchair. "I lost a lot of people I thought would be beside me forever when my health problems started progressing. I never imagined I'd find an all new group of people who would make me laugh so hard, give me shit, and keep me grateful for every day. You guys are the best. Merry Christmas!"

"Merry Christmas!" everyone chimed in and clinked their glasses again.

"Oh hell," Richard said. "I might as well say something too."

Ginny shot an amused glance at Eliza. It was a small thing, but implied a closeness that Present Eliza ached to have.

Richard clumsily pushed back his chair and wobbled to his feet, holding his glass aloft.

"This is a proper toast, to the two beautiful women seated here with me. You make the other fellas down at the retirement village so jealous. They don't have what it takes to get invited to the homes of dazzling women half their age. Oh, and that reminds me. I brought some mistletoe with me. We'll have to put that up after dinner." He winked at both women, prompting playful eye rolls and giggles.

Richard was halfway back to sitting before he popped up again. "Oh, and it's nice to have you join us too, Steven. Although you're not nearly as gorgeous as these two, but I won't hold it against you."

Steven raised his glass a little higher. "I appreciate that."

There was another round of clinking and sipping and then Steven tentatively got to his feet.

"Well, I can't be the odd man out here. Thank you Ginny, for inviting me along and Eliza for welcoming me into your home. Richard, sorry I'm not as lovely as these two, but I hope I'll be pleasant company anyway."

Richard shrugged. "So far, so good."

"Merry Christmas everyone. And now, let's eat!" Steven finished his toast and sat back down.

"Let's eat!" the group echoed, clinking glasses once more and then got started filling their plates.

After the initial lull of passing dishes and spooning out food, Richard turned his attention to Steven.

"Steven," he said, before swallowing a mouthful of green bean casserole, "I'm usually the only lucky male at these gatherings with Eliza and Ginny. Tell us how you came to join our illustrious group."

Steven glanced at Ginny before answering.

"I'm the newest writing professor at the university. Ginny and I are two of the few faculty members that don't take ourselves too seriously so we got along right away. She graciously invited me along to your Christmas dinner when she heard my sad story about being alone in a new town for the holiday."

Ginny grinned and wiggled her eyebrows at Eliza, even though Steven didn't seem to notice.

"Ah. And why are you alone in a new town?" Richard continued, merrily chewing a bite of turkey as he asked.

This time Steven cast a shy look in Eliza's direction before he answered.

"I'm from Connecticut and moved out here for the job. My wife and I split up a few years ago. Our kids are grown and moved on now so I realized there was nothing holding me to the area anymore. Figured it might be good to start fresh somewhere. The posting came up on a job site as a potential match and I figured that was as good a sign as any. So here I am."

"Well," Ginny said, patting Steven's arm. "You aren't alone anymore. You're officially one of us now and part of our goofy little family."

"I really appreciate that, and you, Eliza," he cast an earnest look at her. "Thank you so much for your warm hospitality."

"We're happy to have you," Eliza assured him. "What classes are you teaching?"

"Intro to poetry and poetry writing classes. You could say poetry is my thing."

"Don't get this one started on poetry," Richard nodded his head toward Eliza. "She's always trying to get me to come to poetry readings at the bookstore. It sounds lovely, I suppose, but I just can't understand the stuff."

Steven laughed. "Yeah, some poetry can be pretty obtuse. That's what turns a lot of people off to it in the first place. I lean toward more accessible poets in my classes, Robert Frost, Amanda Gorman, Paul McGlynn,

Lang Leav, and my personal favorite, Jasmine Weathersby."

Eliza felt her own eyes grow large, even if she couldn't quite see how Future Eliza's face reacted to the news.

Future Eliza put down her fork.

"Jasmine Weathersby is my absolute favorite!" she exclaimed. "I have every book she's written."

A broad smile crossed Steven's face.

"Really? I'm so glad to hear that. I don't run into a lot of fans of hers."

"Oh, she's just the best!" Eliza gushed. "Her poems look deceptively simple, but she's able to capture so much emotion in so few words. Reading her work is like..."

"Magic," Steven and Eliza both filled in at the same time.

Ginny shared a meaningful look with Richard, who nodded slightly and stuffed his mouth full of sweet potatoes.

"I had a feeling you two would get each other," Ginny said, looked very satisfied with herself.

"Ah, well. We won't bore you with poetry talk right now. Maybe we can save that for another time?" Steven looked at Eliza as if asking permission.

"I'm up for poetry talk anytime," she agreed. "Especially about Jasmine Weathersby."

The group fell into companionable conversation as they finished eating.

Finally, Richard kicked back and rubbed his belly.

"Mmm, mmm! Everything was delicious. I don't think I'll have to eat again for a week."

Ginny laughed. "Until an hour or two rolls by and we break into the dessert."

Steven groaned. "I'm with Richard. I don't know if I'll be able to do it."

Eliza took a sip of her water and smiled. "Oh, we'll all be able to do it. It's part of the magic of the holidays."

"Speaking of holiday magic," Ginny looked eagerly around the table. "How about we digest a little while we get down to business."

Steven looked at her quizzically.

"White elephant time!" Ginny exclaimed.

Richard plunked an elbow on the table and leaned his forehead on his hand. "Ugh," he groaned. "Must we resort to the exchanging of junk?"

"Which gift did Richard bring? I don't want that one," Ginny teased.

"Speak for yourself!" Eliza interjected. "I have a great gift. I'm excited to see what I end up with."

Steven glanced at everyone else then held up his hands.

"I may have misunderstood the assignment," he said. "I thought it was just supposed to be some extra thing laying around the house–"

Eliza jumped in. "No, you got that right. Whatever you brought will be perfect." They held eye contact for a little longer than necessary, before looking away with shy smiles.

Ginny maneuvered her powerchair out from the dining room and toward the Christmas tree in the living room. Now that her attention had been directed there,

Present Eliza noticed that there were exactly four gifts under the tree.

Richard grunted and groaned his way into a standing position. Eliza smiled and slipped her arm through his.

"Escort me to the Christmas tree, handsome," she said in a playful, husky tone.

Richard regarded her with a wicked grin. "I know what you're up to."

"Oh?"

"Yes, and flattery will get you everywhere. Let's be discreet around Ginny though. Wouldn't want her to think she's lost her chance."

"Friends walk arm in arm. She won't suspect a thing." Eliza planted a quick kiss on Richard's cheek, causing his eyes to go wide.

"Slow down there, girl! I'm an old man after all."

Eliza only giggled and surreptitiously acted as a balance as she led Richard into the next room.

Present Eliza was, once again, struck by the easy camaraderie among this lovely group. She couldn't help but wonder how on earth they'd all come to know one another, or why her future self wasn't with Jacob and the kids for this holiday. That was a possibility she didn't want to linger on.

Once everyone got settled in the living room, Eliza crouched down to pull out the gifts.

"All right!" she exclaimed. "Four lovely gifts for four lovely people. Who should make the first selection?"

"Beauty before age!" Ginny cried.

"Oh, yes. Of course," Richard agreed. "Ladies first. Ginny, go ahead."

Ginny rubbed her hands together like an evil genius.

"I've got my eye on that one!" She pointed to a shoebox sized gift wrapped in red foil paper and embellished with a gold bow and ribbon.

"Man!" Steven called, getting into the spirit of things. "That's the one I was looking at."

"Ha!" Ginny snatched up the present and clutched it to her chest. "Finders keepers! Unless, of course, it's crap, then I'll be happy to trade."

"Let's see if it's as good as it looks," Eliza encouraged.

"It's almost a shame to ruin the wrapping job. Whoever did this has mad wrapping skills." Ginny ran her finger over the smooth paper. No one said a word to own up to it, so she set to work.

"Go big, or go home, right?" She clawed through the paper right in the middle, rather than doing the reserved adult unwrapping shtick. Shiny red scraps littered the ground around her and she was left holding a shoebox. Putting it up to her ear, she shook it. The only sound was a dull thudding. It didn't give anything away.

"This better not be a pair of shoes."

"Get it over with. We're all on tenterhooks here." Richard looked like he was trying to swallow a grin and not really managing it.

Ginny rolled her eyes, but started to take the top off the box. Once she'd gotten it off and parted the tissue paper inside, she burst into raucous laughter.

"You're a bastard!" she wheezed between laughs. "Whoever brought this. You're an absolute bastard!"

Eliza reached up and tipped the box toward her so

she could see what on earth had provoked such a reaction.

A pair of rubber garden clogs toppled out. Not only were they garden clogs in an unreasonably large size, but they were patterned with cartoon cows and chickens.

"You're welcome!" Richard shouted over the laughter. "You're an ingrate, but you're welcome."

"What the hell, Richard?" Ginny wiped tears from her eyes from laughing so hard. "Where did you get these horrible things?"

"A gift giver does not disclose his secrets."

Steven and Eliza exchanged amused glances as all this was going on. Then Eliza motioned to Steven.

"Why don't you go ahead and pick one?"

Steven shook his head. "No, no," he insisted. "We already decided ladies first. You're next."

"But I'm the host. I should go last."

Steven remained firm. "All the more reason to go next."

Eliza's cheeks pinkened a little as she turned her attention to the remaining packages.

"Well," she said, "This one is distinctly book shaped. I can't pass that up."

By then, Richard and Ginny had settled down, although Ginny kept glancing at her new clogs, which would cause a new round of snickering.

"Don't get your hopes up," Steven said, but Eliza was too busy tucking into her chosen bookish-vibes gift.

Once the paper was off, she stared at the item in her hands in complete shock.

"I probably should have brought something else," Steven apologized.

"No," Eliza interrupted. "This couldn't be more perfect. Look!" She held up the book for all to see.

"*Eliza's Dream* by Steven Marlowe," Richard read aloud. "I daresay that gift was definitely intended for you."

"And it's an ARC!" Eliza exclaimed. "It says it doesn't even come out until the spring."

No one had noticed that Ginny's lower jaw had dropped practically to her lap as she pointed an accusing finger at Steven.

"I didn't know you were a writer!"

Steven's cheeks reddened again. It seemed to be an affliction he and Eliza were passing back and forth.

"I thought it was just supposed to be a no pressure, grab something you don't need and pass it off as a gift. I didn't mean for it to be pretentious—"

"No, no!" Eliza said again, hugging the book to her chest. "I love it. The title is perfect. Ginny didn't tell me she was bringing a famous poet to my party!"

"That's because I didn't know!" Ginny exclaimed.

Steven shook his hands. "Oh no. I'm definitely just a lowly little poet. No one knows me."

"Let me see that!" Ginny thrust her hand out for the book, which Eliza passed over.

"Liar!" Ginny shouted. "It says right here on the cover, '*Eliza's Dream* is an ethereal sophomore collection from the author of *These Slow Common Days*.' This is your second book! Someone knows you."

Richard started to cough and waved his hand in Eliza's direction.

"Water," he choked out.

Eliza sprang up. "Of course!" She dashed toward the kitchen.

"I'll help," Steven exclaimed and quickly followed after her.

Once alone in the kitchen, Eliza grabbed a glass out of the cupboard and Steven spoke rapidly.

"I didn't mean anything by it. I wasn't even thinking that your name is Eliza when I wrapped it up."

"No, really," Eliza tried to assure him as she ran cold water into the glass. "It's perfect. I'm excited to read it."

"Well, don't read it with any great expectations. It doesn't compare to Jasmine's work at all."

"Writers are their own worst critics. I already know I'll like your book. And I'm not just saying that. Sometimes I just get this feeling when I hold a book. Like it's the right set of words at the right moment in time. I felt that jolt just now."

"Obviously, as an English professor, I've met other book lovers before, but no one has ever said that happens to them too. I thought I was the only one."

Watching them stop and regard each other, Present Eliza felt like time had stopped. There was something between these two. Like the feeling Future Eliza had just described, Present Eliza could tell this was an important meeting between kindreds. She wanted to break through whatever space/time continuum she was in and talk to Steven about Jasmine's work and poetry in general. She couldn't wait to hear what he had to say.

"Eliza Marie!" Ginny called from the other room. "Did you forget Richard's dying out here? How long does a glass of water take?"

"Not dying!" Richard's garbled voice called. "Just a tickle."

"Coming!" Eliza announced shaking off the moment. "We have a lot more to talk about," she said as she started walking toward the living room. "You'll also have to sign that book for me. It's not every day I get to have dinner with a famous poet."

The scene began to darken like stage lights fading down.

Present Eliza had chills skittering across the surface of her flesh. She was glad Richard was all right, of course, but she was deeply shaken by the fast connection she saw forming between her future self and Steven. Although they'd obviously just met, it was one of those rare soul deep connections that can spark with people. It was heavily charged with Steven, but the dynamics of the whole group was breathtaking to her as well. The camaraderie was so easy. Each of them clearly felt comfortable just being their true selves. No embarrassment. No judgment. Just love. That was the sort of interaction she thought only existed in fiction, but this was proof that it could be possible in real life. If only she found the right path to get to it.

The pinpricks of light appeared around her again.

"Oh no!" she exclaimed. "I was having a lovely time. Do I have to leave already?"

There was no verbal answer, but the pinpricks expanded into white lines again and Eliza understood that she was heading back to her reality.

The next thing she knew, she was sitting on the edge of her guest room bed. The darker orb of the future spirit was just where she'd seen it last, near the Scrooge print.

"What am I supposed to do with that?" Eliza asked, feeling exasperated. Her emotions were tangled in a Gordian knot.

"I don't know what you mean," the weird Future voice said.

"I really liked those people, but what about my family? I didn't see Jacob or my kids in that future. Where were they? How far in the future was that? I need to know more."

"There is no more to tell. It is only one possible future out of countless pathways. How you get there and where it leaves the ones you know now is only up to you and the choices you make."

"Then why show me? Why pick that one particular possibility if the chances are so low I'd actually get there? What does this mean?"

"I have no more to offer. How you act on the things you've seen is up to you."

Eliza groaned, put her elbows on her thighs and her head in her hands.

"Convenient isn't it? Somehow all the decisions come back to me, don't they? Well, I'm tired of figuring everything out, Future. How am I supposed to know what's right?"

The dark orb began to fade from sight.

"I trust you do know. You just have to trust yourself, too."

The Future's unearthly voice faded away but echoed in Eliza's mind.

She wanted to scream. She'd learned so much from

her three visitors, but what was she supposed to do with all this information? What action was she supposed to take? It was so much easier for Scrooge. He'd been a monster, an enemy to all mankind. It wasn't hard to figure out he was supposed to become generous and caring. Eliza's life wasn't so cut and dry.

She let herself switch positions to fall backward onto the bed. Something hard jammed into her lower back. She rolled onto her side and patted around with her hand to figure out what she'd fallen onto.

As soon as her fingers made contact with the edge of the item, she knew. A book.

Her heart started racing and she sat up and felt around for the lamp on the nightstand. After fumbling around for what felt like far too long, she found the switch and flicked on the light.

She could hardly believe what she was holding. It was the advance copy of *Eliza's Dream*!

She quickly flipped open the cover as a shockwave passed through her. It was signed. Somehow she'd gotten the book after Steven had signed it. She ran her fingers over the words inscribed there, feeling the indentation the pen tip had made in the soft paper.

To Eliza: My best friend that I've just met. Make your dreams count. - Steven

Unlike Scrooge after his spirit visitors, Eliza felt completely spent. Seeing the inscription from Steven, knowing everything she'd seen, heard, and felt was real, the only reaction she had was to clutch the book to her chest and sob. She cried for the past she'd left behind, the present that wasn't what she'd imagined, and the unknown future stretching before her. She heard Fran's parting words in her mind, "It's always a choice." Even though she hadn't felt like she had many choices in the last few years, she now understood that wasn't true. It was all a choice. Every day was a series of new choices.

There were a lot of new choices in front of her now. So many directions she could take.

It was still the middle of the night. Eliza knew she wouldn't sleep. There were too many options to consider. Too many epiphanies to process. She didn't know what she was going to do, but she understood the choice was hers, and hers alone.

✿ 5 ✿
ENDING ONE
REMEMBER THE PAST

There was no weak light creeping in through the bottom of the blinds when Eliza heard Derby screeching. It was Christmas morning with a little kid. Despite the shrillness of his tone, Eliza smiled. She remembered her journey with Fran, just a few hours earlier, but it already felt like a lifetime ago. She was vastly changed from the frazzled woman she'd been when she arrived at Edward and Dymond's. Deep inside she'd known it would take something big to jar her from the frantic merry-go-round of her life, and this night had been more than big. Monumental was closer to the right word, but still not strong enough.

Instead of dreading Derby's behavior, she found herself excited to spend one more Christmas with a youngster tearing into his toys with reckless abandon, laughing and shouting over the little things that made children so very happy. It had been a good idea to spend the holiday with Edward, Dymond, and Derby. She never would have expected to feel this way, but a weight had been lifted from her chest. It had also been a good decision to spend the night alone in the guest room. Her act of anger and hurt had resulted in something good and she was immensely grateful for it.

She quietly got out of bed and tiptoed over to the Scrooge picture. Pressing her fingertips ever so slightly to the frame, she took a deep breath.

"You were right, Ebenezer," she whispered. "Thank you so much for sending me the spirits. For everything they taught me. I don't think you just saved me, you've saved my family."

Nothing was amiss with the picture. Scrooge stayed at his counting table, his skin that sickly, miserly, green. The picture may never move again, but it had once. Eliza knew it, and that was enough.

She hadn't packed her bathrobe, so she pulled a decorative fleece blanket off the foot of the bed and wrapped herself in it before leaving the room.

No one else seemed to be stirring, just Derby and presumably his mother. Eliza had the feeling that Edward wouldn't be joining them by the tree until he was good and ready. The bastard.

Eliza's mind was buzzing. She had a lot of damage to repair. It was hard to know what she should do first.

Remembering the time, it seemed wise to stick with the people who were already awake. Odds were she'd get a better response from them than waking anyone else up, so she padded down the hall following the sound of Derby's screeches.

She reached the entrance to the grand living room, the same scene as her blow up. Derby was standing beside the tree thrusting his hands toward the presents.

"Open now!" he bellowed.

Dymond sat on the floor by the tree. She didn't look like an Instagram post now. She wore a ratty bathrobe and her perfect hair was in disarray. Those cascading waves she'd sported the day before were a tangled mess now. This was the sort of woman Eliza could envision being friends with. Someone who was real, flawed, not living her best life every minute of every day.

Remembering what those early parenthood days were like, she was amazed that Dymond ever looked put together at all. It occurred to her that just because Dymond was young, it didn't mean that everything was easier for her. She now knew that her marriage certainly wasn't easy. Dymond was hiding a lot of secrets too, like Eliza. She just managed to hide them behind a glossy exterior that looked like happiness and success.

"No, baby," Dymond said in a croaky, sleep-laced voice. "It's the middle of the night. Everyone else is sleeping. We have to wait until they wake up."

"Santa came!" Derby gestured wildly at the mounds of presents surrounding the tree. "Time to open!"

"Not yet. We have to wait, okay?"

Derby stomped his foot, getting ready to descend into meltdown mode, when Eliza got an idea. She knocked gently on the archway into the room, startling both Dymond and Derby.

"Excuse me," Eliza said. "I'm so sorry to intrude, but I was looking for a helper to make a special Christmas treat with me. Does anyone here know where I could find a helper?"

Dymond cocked her head quizzically, and Derby

turned away from the presents to contemplate the question.

"What kind of helper?" he asked, his little kid voice laced with skepticism.

Eliza couldn't let up now that she had a little momentum.

"Oh, someone small and smart and who probably likes frosting a lot."

Derby's eyes went the size of saucers as he contemplated frosting.

"That's me!" he exclaimed. "I eat the frosting!"

"Whoa! That's perfect! But I need you to paint with the frosting too. Do you think you can do that?"

Derby started to jump up and down enthusiastically and Dymond looked stricken.

Eliza put her hands out to try to bring all the emotions down.

"Ok, first, we have to be really quiet, ok? We're like elves doing a secret project for Santa, right? We don't want to wake up the others and ruin the surprise."

Derby stopped jumping and closed his mouth tight.

Next, she turned to Dymond.

"Listen, I'm really sorry about my outburst last night. I was frustrated and things have been building up with the holidays, school winding down for break, dealing with my mom and Edward's joke just made me snap–"

"No," Dymond shook her head and wrapped herself tighter in her bathrobe. "I should be apologizing about that. Edward was way out of line. You had every right to be upset. And I wasn't paying attention to Derby. I should have jumped in right away–"

"You know what? Let's just put it all in the past and leave it there. We got this holiday off on the wrong foot, but maybe we can start it fresh right now. With a batch of Christmas cookies?"

Derby looked like he was going to start jumping and shouting again, so Eliza put her finger to her lips lightning fast.

"Quiet as elves, remember?" she whispered.

Derby clapped his pudgy toddler hands over his mouth and nodded.

"Ok. So how about if we tiptoe into the kitchen and start baking?"

"You don't have to do this," Dymond said, coming up close to Eliza and leaning in so Derby wouldn't hear. "You're a guest. You should be sleeping at this hour."

Eliza shrugged. "Can't sleep anyway. Let's just say, it's been a night."

Dymond didn't argue with that.

The unlikely team of three made their way to the kitchen. Eliza channeled the old days when her kids used to like helping her. Luckily, she knew her preferred sugar cookie recipe by heart. The only thing she didn't know was her way around Edward and Dymond's kitchen. She was grateful Dymond had decided to tag along and join the fun.

Dymond got all the mixing bowls, utensils, measuring cups, and ingredients together. She also retrieved Derby's little step stool from the bathroom so he could reach the counter. Eliza made Derby the designated frosting elf and showed him how to stir up butter and sugar to make a gloppy frosting. It didn't matter to her if the end product was Insta-worthy or not, and for once, it seemed like Dymond was content to enjoy the moment in real time and not worry about what an unknown audience might think.

While the first batch of cookies was in the oven, and Derby was content playing around with frosting, Eliza decided to make another attempt at real conversation with Dymond.

"You know," she said quietly, "It was really nice of you and Edward to invite us over for Christmas. It's a big undertaking to host a holiday. Thank you."

Dymond absently finger combed her hair before she answered.

"You know, I kinda wanted to prove that I could do it. I feel like people don't take me seriously a lot of the time and I just wanted to pull this off and make a nice holiday for everyone. We see how that's going so far." She scoffed at herself and pulled her hair back with her hands, even though she didn't have an elastic handy to secure it with. "I didn't even think to make Christmas cookies."

This was the deepest conversation she'd ever managed to have with Dymond. Whether it was the effect of the spirits, her outburst, the conversation she knew Dymond and Edward had had, or the early hour, Eliza was grateful it was finally happening.

"Trust me," Eliza jumped in, "I don't remember to do everything either. There's so much to do and there's all this pressure to do everything perfectly. It's too much, and it can suck your joy away if you let it. You saw. I was pretty joyless yesterday."

Dymond gave a low chuckle. "Yeah. Same. I thought

the cocktails would spread some Christmas cheer but I think it actually unleashed Christmas angst."

Eliza shrugged. "Mine was delicious though. You make a mean chocolate martini."

"Thanks." Dymond didn't sound too convinced, but at least they were making progress. It hadn't been a long conversation, but it was a start.

Before she could try to keep conversation flowing, the oven timer dinged, signifying that it was time to get the cookies out and cooling. Eliza looked around, realizing she didn't know where the oven mitts were.

"What do you need?" Dymond asked.

"Oven mitts?"

"Oh right!" Dymond went to a drawer and pulled out two perfectly white oven mitts that looked like they'd never been used once. So Dymond wasn't a happy little homemaker who spent her days baking. Big deal. If Eliza was being honest, she didn't exactly love baking herself. Just the yearly Christmas cookies which had become her thing. Other than that, she thought it was so much hassle. She'd rather eat baked goods than make them. Apparently that was something else she had in common with Dymond.

Shortly after the cookies came out of the oven, Derby and Dymond started frosting and sprinkling them. Eliza looked up from mixing the next batch of dough and saw Bella standing in the doorway.

"Oh!" Eliza exclaimed. "Merry Christmas! I didn't know you were up, too."

"Who can sleep when the house smells like fresh cookies?"

Judging by who was not in the kitchen, all males ages fifteen or over could sleep no matter what.

"Need any help?" Bella asked.

Those were words that hadn't come out of Bella's mouth in longer than Eliza could remember. Her heart warmed as she remembered seeing Bella's little girl face shine with joy when she opened the dollhouse from her grandpa. It was hard to remember sometimes, but that sweet little girl was still inside her teenage daughter. The circumstances just had to be right for her to show up.

"I'm doing sprinkles!" Derby exclaimed, shaking a small hill of them onto his current cookie.

"Actually," Eliza said, as an idea popped into her head. "Would you mind taking over with this dough? There's something else I need to do real quick."

"Sure." Bella stepped in and took the spoon from her mother. "I didn't think we were going to have cookies for breakfast this year. This is a nice surprise."

"You can't eat cookies for breakfast!" Derby laughed like Bella was being silly.

"Oh yeah?" Bella asked him with a sly smile playing at her lips. "Who says?"

"Mom!" Derby shouted, pointing a heavily frosted finger at Dymond.

"Yes," Dymond smiled, mussing up his hair. "We know that cookies for breakfast isn't healthy. Our body needs good fuel for the day, doesn't it?"

"Most days, yes," Bella agreed. "But Christmas is special. Sometimes you get to bend the rules for special days."

Eliza washed her hands in the sink and smiled to

herself as she listened to her daughter, in good humor for a change, extol the virtues of Christmas cookie breakfast.

Slipping out of the kitchen, Eliza made her way back to the guest room she was meant to have shared with Jacob. She hesitated for only a moment before composing herself to open the door. She pushed it open a crack and listened...nothing but the low snores of her sleeping husband. Apparently, he'd been out like a light all night long. How he managed it, she'd never know, but she was in much higher spirits than the day before so it didn't make her mad.

She didn't want to wake him until she was good and ready, so she crept into the room and very quietly closed the door behind her. In her mind's eye, she was back at the Christmas when she was pregnant with Bella. If she wanted to stay connected to her husband, she'd have to do her part to initiate what she wanted. She wasn't going to do everything all the time. It felt like that's what she had been doing. But they weren't going to get any closer if Jacob kept coming home at the end of the day wanting to fool around before bed, and Eliza feeling like she'd been emotionally neglected and ignored all day while managing everyone else's needs. Maybe if she initiated the fun things she wanted to do to feel appreciated and seen, they could enjoy the benefits together. It was worth a try anyway.

Neither had been so busy and distracted before the kids. Jacob had picked up his guitar to sing Christmas songs with her then. Eliza couldn't play any instruments, but she could sing. She cleared her throat and then started singing in a low voice, "The first Noel..."

Jacob didn't stir.

"The angel did say..."

With each line, she became a little louder and a little more confident.

By the time she reached the end of the first chorus, Jacob snuffled back to the land of wakefulness, rubbed his eyes, and squinted at his singing wife.

She stopped singing once she'd gotten his attention.

"Merry Christmas," she said.

"Merry Christmas," Jacob returned. "What's going on?"

Eliza tentatively sat at the very corner of the bed.

"Well, it's Christmas morning and I finally had a nice stretch of alone time to think."

Jacob propped himself up on his elbows.

"Ok," he answered cautiously.

"First, I'm sorry for making a scene yesterday. I shouldn't have blown up like that, but honestly, I'm wearing very thin between work, dealing with my mother, keeping track of all the kid's stuff and it just pushed me over the edge when I was already frustrated for having to text with my mom and then Edward said that—"

"Hey," Jacob pushed himself all the way up to sitting. "I know you have a lot going on. Edward shouldn't have said what he said. It was really disrespectful."

"So why didn't you say anything? You didn't jump in to defend me at all and that felt almost as bad as what he said in the first place."

Jacob rubbed his face and snorted.

"Why didn't I say anything? Ironically, because I

didn't want to make a scene. I thought you'd let it roll off your back and the conversation would die."

That's what she usually did, get walked all over. Get pushed and pulled and twisted until her own feelings weren't even worth anything anymore. No wonder she was becoming detached and anxious. She wasn't replenishing herself, just like all the women's magazines and blog articles said: "self-care isn't selfish." It may not be selfish, but it doesn't mean it fits into the schedule either. It also doesn't mean other people will grant the time and space to do it more than once in a blue moon.

"Well, I can't take it anymore. My bullshit barrel is full and more comes along faster than I can empty any of it out. I was already over capacity and then Edward pushed and I blew up. I think that's going to happen a lot more unless I get more time, regularly, to be a human. Just me. Eliza. Not Bella and Bobby's mom. Not Jillian's daughter. Not Jacob's wife. Not the event coordinator at the bookstore."

"That sounds great."

"I know it sounds great, but it doesn't mean that all of you let the messes of life pile up while I'm trying to recharge. I don't want to take an hour bath and come out to find more problems than when I went in. The kids have to step up and do more for themselves. It's past time they take more responsibility. You need to stand in and make the decisions when I'm doing something else. Even my mom. She's old, but she's not a little kid. If it isn't an emergency, she can't expect me to drop everything I'm already doing to do her bidding. It's too much. I can't do it all."

"Ok. That sounds good. We'll talk to the kids, and

your mom, and we'll all pay better attention to what we can take off your plate. I don't want you to feel like you have to do it all."

Eliza had expected some pushback, but she was pleasantly surprised to feel like she and Jacob were a team again. Like those early days. Them against the world.

"I want to have fun too," she continued. "Remember before Bella was born? That Christmas Eve you brought out the guitar and we sang Christmas carols together? I want to do things like that again. Just me and you."

Jacob smiled. "Wow, yeah. I'd forgotten about that."

"What even happened to your guitar? You haven't played it in years."

"I think it's in the basement somewhere. I didn't know you missed it."

"I didn't know I missed it either, but I do."

The two sat in companionable silence for a few moments. It was comfortable in a way she hadn't felt for quite some time.

Finally, Jacob looked around. "What time is it anyway?"

He found the clock and discovered it was now 5:30 a.m.

"C'mon," Jacob said. "Why don't we go back to bed for a while. It's way too early to be up."

"I left Bella, Dymond, and Derby in the kitchen. We were making our traditional cookie breakfast."

"Hmmm," Jacob said, scratching his chin. "I remember you saying you wanted everyone to step up. Sounds like the three of them can handle making some cookies while you get started on relaxing more."

Eliza felt the unconscious tension in her chest uncoil. She was so used to hanging on to everything, she hadn't thought it might be difficult to let go. Although, as she watched Jacob turn down the blankets on her usual side of the bed, she suddenly wanted nothing more than to cuddle up in bed and let someone else carry the torch of making the magic.

She stood up, dropped the throw blanket she'd been carrying around, and happily snuggled into the warm nest Jacob had created for them. He cuddled up next to her and wrapped her in a gentle hug. It was her favorite kind. No expectation. No demands. Just a physical act of solidarity and connection.

He kissed her neck and nestled his cheek on her shoulder.

"I love you, Eliza," he said.

"I love you too, Jacob."

As Eliza closed her eyes, she was pleased to realize that she really meant it. It wasn't a magical change, and she didn't expect everything to be perfect from now on, but it was the beginning of a new start. And for the first time in a long time, she felt ready to see what the rest of her day would hold...but after she got a little sleep.

6

ENDING TWO

MAKING THE PRESENT

There was no way to know how long Eliza had laid on her back, contemplating everything she'd seen and heard with her supernatural visitors. Although all three visitors had given her much to think about, she kept coming back to the present. Her kids, who still needed her, even appreciated her, although they didn't overtly show it. Her unusual sister-in-law who wanted to forge a relationship with her, in the midst of her own difficult marriage. Eliza's own marriage angst. Her complicated relationship with her mother. There were still so many roles to juggle and expectations to fill, but the night had changed her. It had been good to step outside of herself and see what was really going on around her. How to react to it all? That was the new question. But for the first time in a long time, she felt like she was in control of the answer to that question. It didn't matter to her whether her mother would be displeased with her choices. She didn't care if Jacob wasn't thrilled by her actions. She didn't mind so much that her kids didn't show her much affection anymore. They were going to be all right and the enormous pressure that relieved was astronomical.

There was only the matter of yesterday's blow up and how she would handle things from there. Clearly, the kids weren't enjoying themselves and would have been happier at home. No question that Eliza would have preferred staying home. Jacob had brought them here, for whatever unknown reason. The clear answer was to excuse themselves, even on Christmas day, and go salvage the present. It did feel icky to leave Dymond with such a jerk, but she wasn't a child. Also, if she wanted to have a relationship with Eliza, she could have done something. Their conversation pre-incident left much to be desired. If she wouldn't take openings to connect when they were offered, it wasn't Eliza's fault.

Eliza realized with growing determination that she just wanted to go home and enjoy the holiday on her own terms. It may be too much to ask of Jacob or her mother, but after the night she'd just had, she didn't care. They weren't living her life. She was. If she didn't make more choices for herself, the magma was just going to rise again and cause another outburst. It would happen more and more frequently and no one would be happy. She was changing, body and mind, and that was reality.

With a new plan forming, she got up and started packing her bag. It might be dramatic, but to hell with it. She'd already endured too much.

Bag packed, and dressed for the day, she glanced at the clock on the nightstand. The glowing red numbers read 5:09 a.m. By the time she got everyone up and moving, Derby would be up to open presents. No matter. They could do a quick present exchange and get the heck out of there.

She grabbed her bag, took a backward glance at the room that had given her the most magical Christmas Eve of her life, and quietly moved into the hallway. Normally, her heart would be hammering away in her chest. She'd be thinking of a million different ways Jacob might respond and how the whole thing would make him feel. Now, she knew even Dymond wasn't having a good time. There were things for Dymond and Edward to sort out and they didn't need houseguests acting as a bandage to cover up the wounds.

She knocked quietly on Jacob's door. No response. Not that she'd expected any. She already knew he'd been sleeping peacefully that night.

The door was unlocked, as she suspected, so she pushed it open and stepped inside. Jacob was, indeed, still snoring away in bed. Her eyes were accustomed to the low light so she could make out the shape of Jacob, starfished wide across the middle of the big bed. Well, good thing she hadn't slept with him. Looked like he needed a vacation from sharing a bed too.

Eliza set her suitcase down beside the door and went to sit on the side of the bed. The mattress was so firm that her sitting didn't so much as jostle Jacob one inch. Subtlety wasn't going to cut it, so she went ahead and shook Jacob's arm until he startled awake.

"What time is it?" he asked, sounding completely groggy.

"After five."

"In the morning?"

"Yes."

"What's wrong?" Jacob sat up, snapping to attention in the face of some possible threat.

Eliza took a deep breath. She might not have the fear and trepidation she once would when delivering news she knew Jacob wouldn't like, but she still didn't relish it.

"I want to go home." It was just a simple declaration. There was no way to misconstrue that.

"What? Now?"

"Well, I'm sure Derby will be up soon wanting to open presents. We can do that since we brought the gifts but I don't want to stay here the rest of the week."

"I already knew that," Jacob said.

"I know, but did you ever consider the reason I didn't want to come?"

She paused and Jacob's lack of response was her answer.

"I didn't want to come because I was afraid Edward would do something aggravating or uncomfortable, just like he did, and I didn't want to spend our holiday walking on eggshells because of it."

Now Jacob sighed. "Your mother does aggravating and uncomfortable things all the time. Do you think I want to spend my free time dealing with her?"

"No, but neither do I. We're at a tough stage of life. I thought having teenagers was going to be a lot easier than having preschoolers but I'm more exhausted mentally and physically than I ever was when they were little. Now I've added in the very real threat of my mom dying any time now. Your parents are off living the good life and my mom is on the slow slide to the end. I hate it. I absolutely hate it. We don't even have a good relationship with Edward and Dymond. He just insulted me, for no reason, and I don't want to stay here so he can continue to pretend he's so much better than us. He isn't. He doesn't treat you any better than he treats me and I don't know why you put up with it."

She wasn't saying anything she hadn't already expressed before. She just hoped this time, maybe Jacob would actually hear her. Unusual things were going on, after all. Maybe this wasn't too much to ask.

Jacob gave a long exhale.

"You really want to leave? On Christmas day? You don't think that'll make things any more tense?"

"Can you look me in the eye and honestly say you're having a good time here?"

Jacob didn't say anything for a long while. Finally, when he did speak, his words were quiet.

"I don't have a good time at home either. If we aren't running around doing something for the kids, we're doing it for your mother. That's not much of a Christmas break to me. Just more of the same. That's why I was excited when Edward invited us over. I wanted to do something different for a change."

The words hit Eliza's core like impact on a tuning fork. He was so right. They did need to do something different, but being awkward at Edward and Dymond's wasn't it.

"Then let's do something fun." Eliza pulled her phone out of her pocket, adrenalin flooding through her as she recalled a vision of the future that she never wanted to come true.

"What are you doing? It's Christmas day. It's too late to plan something now."

Eliza shook her head as the idea gathered traction.

"It's never too late," Eliza said, actually believing it. "There's always something that doesn't get booked up."

"Well yeah, that's the crappy stuff. But what do you mean 'booked up?' We can't just leave here and take a trip."

"Why not? People take last minute trips all the time. Look at your parents."

"We don't! And where is the money going to come from? Everything will be at least double the price just because it's Christmas. That doesn't fit into the financial plan at all."

Eliza winced, thinking about how her outlook on money, that she thought was purely practical, was robbing her family of shared experiences. She didn't want to be that rigid about money anymore.

"Look! Here!" Eliza held out her phone showing Jacob the vacant rental home she just found at Islamorada. Jacob had wanted to visit the Florida Keys forever, but there had always been an excuse not to go. Now, they both wanted to get away, so why not do it?

"Have you lost your mind?" Jacob turned from the glow of the phone to Eliza's expectant face. "We can't just decide on a whim that today's the day we finally go to the Keys. Besides, flight prices are going to be sky high today."

The words made sense, but after the night Eliza had just experienced, she wasn't in the mood for playing it safe and predictable. Their lives needed a shakeup, in a positive way for a change, and this idea was sounding better by the second.

"You know what? I don't care. Things are only going to get harder before they get easier, right? It's not like my mom's going to start getting younger and stronger. Once something happens, it's going to be a decline and then we're really not going to be able to do anything. We both have the time off right now. We do have the money. Remember that money we got when my grandma died? It's been sitting in savings in case we needed it fast. I think we just found out what we need it for."

"Eliza, this isn't responsible. What if something goes wrong with the cars or the house? We can always use more money for the kids' college accounts. We already have this money socked away in case of emergency. Vacation doesn't count as an emergency."

Eliza couldn't be derailed.

"What if we have a heart attack or get into a car accident next week and we can never go to the Keys? I'm not saying we run off and take a trip every month. You can't say things haven't been stressful and hectic lately. What's wrong with being impulsive and doing something for us once? Can't you just close your eyes for a minute and imagine how good it will feel to unwind on the beach?"

Eliza closed her own eyes and she could see it all, plain as the visits she'd had with the spirits. Sitting on the porch of a little yellow beach house, listening to the waves crash and recede from the shore. Seagulls calling. The invigorating scent of the salt water on the ocean breeze. Yes, yes! She more than wanted to take this spontaneous trip. She needed it. They all needed it.

When she opened her eyes again, she saw that Jacob's eyes were still closed, but there was a lazy smile on his face.

Finally, Eliza came up with one last idea to push him over the edge.

"We can open gifts with everybody this morning. Derby will probably be up soon anyway. We can make out like this was the Christmas gift I got you all along. We came here, but I never said anything because I didn't want to spoil the surprise. Then it doesn't look like we're leaving because of last night."

Jacob scratched his neck. "Are you thinking we take the kids or leave them here?"

Tempting as it was to ditch the kids, Eliza couldn't do that to them. They barely knew Dymond, Edward was a jerk, and Derby was...a bit much.

"The kids could use a break too, but maybe we can plan to do something for our anniversary next year. Even just a weekend away. The kids are more than old enough to hold down the fort for a few days."

"Who are you and what have you done with Eliza?"

Eliza grinned, thinking of all she'd learned from her supernatural visitors.

"Let's just say I had a lot to think about last night and it's high time we put a little more sparkle into our marriage." She held up her hands and wiggled her fingers. "Surprise!"

"So, we're seriously doing this? We're flying to the Florida Keys...today? With no summer clothes in our bags?"

142

Surprisingly, that didn't bother Eliza either. "We're doing it. We've got enough underwear for the week. We can each buy a couple cheap t-shirts, shorts, and swimsuits. The rental house has a washer and dryer. We can do laundry. It's no big deal."

Jacob shook his head, still incredulous, but not fighting the uncharacteristic suggestion anymore.

"Are there even flights today from here?"

"You find out. I'll wake up the kids and tell them to pack. Best to be ready so we can catch whatever flight is available."

As Eliza was about to jump up and make for the door, Jacob grabbed her wrist.

"You've never been sexier. Just so you know."

Eliza laughed. She felt pretty sexy, but more so, powerful and free. For the first time in a very long time, she was grabbing her present and making it what she wanted. She wasn't fulfilling the roles she was used to playing. She was too busy being Eliza. At least she knew it was in her, and it was something she'd have to do far more often.

She roused the kids, who were more than excited to enjoy a tropical holiday away when they'd expected a boring time in Ohio with relatives they didn't particularly like. In fact, she couldn't say when she'd ever seen her teens leap out of bed and get to work so fast. While they were busy packing and dressing, Eliza crept back to see if Jacob had found a flight that was leaving relatively soon. The less time she had to continue pretending to have fun at Edward and Dymond's the better.

"You're sure you really want to do this?" Jacob asked, looking at her while holding his phone.

"Of course I do," Eliza said, flopping down next to him again. "I couldn't want anything more."

"Okay then. This is it." Jacob made a show of slowly pressing a "pay now" button on his screen. A confirmation code from Delta Airlines showed up and he tilted his phone toward Eliza.

"Plane takes off in three hours," he said. "We should be at the airport in about an hour to be safe."

"Perfect!" Eliza leaned toward Jacob and gave him a kiss on the cheek. "This is going to be the best Christmas of our lives!"

"Hold your horses," Jacob said. "I just booked a flight. I didn't book a place to stay yet."

Normally, such a slapdash trip would be the stuff of nightmares, but now that it was happening, Eliza was exhilarated. There was nothing that could break her mood, especially not logistics.

"That's still on my phone. I'll book it. Although, I'd sleep on a public beach in a lounge chair if I had to. At least we'll finally be in the Keys. No more excuses."

"Seriously," Jacob said, pinning Eliza with a hard stare. "What has gotten into you?"

Eliza considered her answer for a moment before it came to her. "Christmas spirit," she said. "I think I've finally got mine back."

7

ENDING THREE

TOWARD THE FUTURE

Eliza's mind was racing from all she'd experienced with the spirits, but her glimpse of the future wouldn't leave her mind. She'd seen two starkly different types of holiday. The dullest Christmas with Jacob haunted her. It was like two strangers had sat down for a bland meal and a poorly planned gift exchange. After twenty-plus years, they should both be doing better than that. They should want to do better, but it didn't seem like either of them cared enough. Their spark was gone. She knew it wasn't inevitable that her marriage would end up like that, but faced with the task of working hard to save it, she knew it would take a lot of energy. The one thing that was rapidly draining from her on a daily basis. Still, she'd have to sit down with Jacob and have a long talk. That wasn't the way she wanted to live the second half of her life. It was painful to watch it secondhand with the spirit, she could imagine how much worse it would feel to have that as reality day in and day out.

They were well overdue for dedicated time together. It would help them decide what path they were on and which path they wanted to pursue.

That beige potential future wasn't the only thing she'd seen though. In complete contrast was the vibrant, boisterous, apartment filled with friendship and laughter. She couldn't shake the zing of excitement she'd felt seeing Ginny, Richard, and Steven.

Ginny was exactly what was missing from her life. The type of friend she thought existed in the minds of authors and screenwriters, but not in real life. How in the world had her future self met Ginny? Or Richard, for that matter? The sarcastic banter he dished out was so steeped in familiarity he must have been part of their group for some time. Had Ginny gathered him into the fold as well? She'd brought Steven along. Maybe she was just one of those magnetic people who had a gift for cultivating friendships. Eliza regretted that the only information she had was a first name, which was likely a nickname, and that she worked in a university somewhere. That wasn't enough to find anyone, and the realization felt as heavy as a weight being pinned to her heart.

Eliza already missed them deeply and she'd only spent a few minutes watching their celebration. Her chest ached with the desire to see them again, talk to them more, and to pick Steven's brain about Jasmine Weathersby's poetry. A zap of electricity tingled down her spine just thinking about what a full conversation with Steven about Jasmine's poetry would be like. He was a university professor and a poet. His perspective would be so rich and knowledgeable. Jacob wasn't into things like that and even the ladies at work weren't poetry fans. She remembered the way Steven's brown eyes had lit up behind his glasses when Future Eliza had mentioned Jasmine's work. They had to have that conversation. It was something she knew she needed to experience.

Thinking of poetry, she hadn't let go of Steven's book since she'd come back to reality. As much as she wanted to read it, she could only clutch it to her chest, like she was hugging a long lost friend. The act grounded her in the knowledge that everything she'd experienced with the spirits had been real. A signed book couldn't appear out of thin air. Steven had really been at some future home of hers, written the book, signed it to her. It was incredible and comforting.

With uninterrupted time to read, she normally would have settled right in with the book, but other than just wanting to hold it and stay close to her brief memory, she was terrified to know what was inside. What if Steven had somehow tapped into her life? Not just her life, her very essence? Perhaps the Eliza in the book was restless and dissatisfied like her. She didn't know how it would feel to read the words of this unknown man if they resonated with her own life. A tingle crawled up her spine and shivered her shoulders. She wanted to know if *Eliza's Dream* was a coincidence or not, but it was too early to discover that. There was too much else to process.

She didn't know what Steven, Richard, and Ginny symbolized for her or how they fit in with her current life. Would she have to leave Jacob in order for that possible future to be true? Were things that far gone that there wasn't anything left worth saving and it was time to part ways and start a new adventure on her own? The thought left her heart pounding in equal parts fear and excitement. What would it be like to be that woman with a boisterous group of friends who looked out for each other? Eliza didn't have fantasies of being swept off her feet by another man, but she did dream of having close friends and being her own person again.

Steven himself was quite a conundrum as well. He was attractive, but more than that, Eliza loved how it had felt to see him. Even though they were strangers, they clearly had a connection. She felt seen in a way she hadn't for years. It was something welcome and fresh at a time in her life when things felt stale, even though chaos was the only predictable thing.

There was always something more important to do for someone else's sake, and her changing body was screaming at her that time was not infinite. She was heading into the second half. The last half. It was a sobering thought.

If she lived as long as she already had, she'd be ninety six years old. Her grandparents hadn't lived that long. It wasn't a thought she wanted to face, but everyone has to sometime.

Perimenopause made sure she realized she was at the demarcation line between her young self and the self that was carrying her onward to old age. Things were serious now in a way they hadn't been before. If she wasn't willing to go out on a limb now and seek the things she really wanted, the chance might literally be gone forever.

Meanwhile, Jacob went on with nary a care about

aging. His entire system wasn't thrown into disorder because his hormones were spiking and dropping at the errant whims of biology. How could he ever understand what it was like to be squeezed by your family, your job, your parents, and even your own damn body? The biggest problem he'd had to face was whether or not he'd be able to maintain an erection if he wanted one. And if he couldn't, lo and behold, he could just scamper off and order himself some little blue pills and problem solved. He was back in the sack and ready to roll. Eliza had been trying to regulate her hormones. Some doctors listened and took her seriously. Others didn't. And that was when she managed to squeeze in an appointment for herself here and there. It was a trial and error for her in a way it wasn't for Jacob, and yes, in a way, it made her resentful. She'd already put in twenty years of managing their social calendar, knowing the kids schedules, taking care of doctor appointments, remembering all the birthdays, anniversaries, and holidays and planning them accordingly. Without the body and mind of her twenties and thirties, she didn't know if she could keep it together anymore. Lately, she wondered if she even wanted to.

She flipped on the bedside light and stared at the book in her hands. *Eliza's Dream* by Steven Marlowe. Steven Marlowe! Now that she was back in her own reality, there was tangible evidence to go on. She could see if this Steven Marlowe existed in her world, and if so, where was he?

Equipped with a full name, Eliza grabbed her phone and did a search for Steven Marlowe. She gasped when his picture popped up with his own website. He didn't have the gray around the temples she'd seen, and his glasses were clear instead of blue, but it was definitely him. The first book he'd written was on the site, *These Slow Common Days*. In fact, she was shocked to discover it had only recently come out. *Eliza's Dream* didn't exist yet.

Feeling those tingles in her spine again, she turned back to the book and flipped to the copyright page. Sure enough, the copyright date was five years in the future.

Eliza felt like she'd been sucker punched. What could that possibly mean? She was holding a book, with her name in the title, by a person she'd met in a possible projection of her future. Was she to become the reason the book was titled as it was, even though Future Eliza hadn't met Steven when he'd written the book? Were they destined to meet all along?

Unable to stop herself, she returned her attention to the website and scrolled to the author biography page. She learned that Steven lived in Connecticut with his wife, Rosea. If the vision came true, in a few years, he wouldn't be married anymore, but this path was already different from that future. There was no telling what might change.

If he was in Connecticut now, he might move in the future. To where, she didn't know. She had no idea where that delightful gathering had taken place, nor which university Ginny and Steven worked at. She couldn't trace Ginny, but she could find Steven. He probably didn't know Ginny yet, but if there was hope of finding any of them, Steven Marlowe was it.

At the bottom of Steven's bio, an innocent green

button offered her the easiest opportunity to change her life.

CONTACT ME.

Overwhelmed, she stuffed both the book and her phone under the pillow and sat on the bed taking deep breaths. What did this all mean? Why would the spirits have shown her this potential future, with these potential friends if she wasn't meant to do anything about it? Surely, the point of the night was to take action, just as Scrooge had taken action. Unlike Scrooge, she'd been given something that defied the laws of time and space. She had visited a possibility and come back with something tangible. A book. With her name on it. Signed by someone who already felt very meaningful to her, although they'd only shared a brief moment together.

Why would she be filled with such longing to spend more time with Steven, Ginny, and Richard if it wasn't supposed to happen? Why did she have the book if she wasn't meant to use the information to forge a pathway to the people she wanted to know?

Fran's words echoed in her ears. Everything was a choice. She wasn't trapped. She didn't have to remain in a frantic life defined by her family's expectations of her. *Eliza's Dream* was offering her the chance to take control of her future and define who she was for herself. She had to take it, otherwise, she knew she'd regret it for the rest of her life.

Palms sweating and heart pounding, she reached under the pillow and pulled her phone and the book back out. She navigated back to the contact form and clicked the button. A blank email template popped up and Eliza got to work.

Dear Mr. Marlowe,

My name is Eliza Skragg and I'm the community events coordinator for Beau's Books in Grand Rapids, Michigan. I would love to set up an author event with you in celebration of your new poetry collection, *These Slow Common Days*. I can offer you a travel stipend and an honorarium for your time and talent. Dates are flexible and I can work with your schedule.

I look forward to the chance to work with you and help bring awareness to you and the brilliant debut work you've crafted.

Sincerely,

Eliza Skragg

She included her email and cell number for good measure and pressed send with a flutter of her heart. If the universe had given her this nudge toward her future, she would not squander it. It was up to Steven and the universe now to see what may come of it. She only hoped he would reply and through their interaction, she'd be able to find Ginny and Richard one day. One step at a time.

High from the anticipation of first contact, Eliza put her phone away and turned back to Steven's book. She ran her hand over the cover as if caressing a priceless artifact. Indeed, it had instantly become one of the most precious gifts she'd ever received.

She opened the book with the intention of reading it, but stopped when she heard the somewhat muffled shrieks of Derby getting up for Christmas morning. The sound brought her back to the here and now of her present reality, but she was no longer annoyed by it. Coming to Edward and Dymond's, the blow up, sleeping in a separate room, all of these things had brought her to exactly where she was supposed to be. She was sure of it. A warm wave of peace washed over her and she smiled, even as Derby hollered again and she heard the loud stomping of little feet heading toward the Christmas tree downstairs.

Suddenly, the urgency to ingest Steven's words and see if there was any wisdom directed at her in his book passed. She stood up and tucked the book into her suitcase, surprised by her newfound calm. She didn't need to see if there was a poetic blueprint for her life inside the pages of Steven's book. She was Eliza Skragg. She would create her own dreams.

A MIDLIFE CHRISTMAS CAROL
PLAYLIST

Blue Sky Action - Above & Beyond
    I Miss You - Blink 182
    1973 - James Blunt
    Beginning to Feel the Years - Brandi Carlile
    Heroes and Songs - Brandi Carlile
    The Joke - Brandi Carlile
    Right on Time - Brandi Carlile
    Re: Love - Cassandra Coleman
    "99" - Barnes Courtney
    What Was I Made For? - Billie Eilish
    Every Shade of Blue - The Head and the Heart
    Virginia (Wind in the Night) - The Head and the Heart
    Pineapple Head - Crowded House
    America's Sweetheart - Elle King
    Furious Rose - Lisa Loeb
    I Lied - Lord Huron
    What Do it Mean - Lord Huron
    Angela - The Lumineers
    Ho Hey - The Lumineers
    Good Old Days - Macklemore
    Midlife - Ordinary Elephant
    Relic of the Rain - Ordinary Elephant
    Everyday is Christmas - Sia
    Eye of the Needle - Sia

Fair Game - Sia
Pin Drop - Sia
Straight for the Knife - Sia
Underneath the Christmas Lights - Sia
Underneath the Mistletoe - Sia
Christmas Lights - Straight No Chaser
Alone Time - Rufus Wainwright
Crumb by Crumb - Rufus Wainwright
This One's for the Ladies - Rufus Wainwright
Unfollow the Rules - Rufus Wainwright

ABOUT THE AUTHOR

Alana Oxford is a Michigan author of romcoms, low spice romance, and humorous women's fiction. She wants her stories to bring sunshine and smiles to her readers. She enjoys improv comedy, moody music, everything book related, and has an ongoing love affair with the United Kingdom.

https://www.sjlomas.com/alana-oxford

"I loved this sweet romance! The chemistry between Seth and Patrice was palpable, and I was rooting for them from the beginning." -Lacie Waldon author of *From the Jump*.

"I couldn't put it down! It was just what I needed, to get lost in a story with characters I couldn't get enough of, taking me on a journey of wild fun and romance." -Allyson Martinek, Morning host 100.3 WNIC and author of *Living On Air*.

Life isn't always a walk in the park, but when Patrice takes her Pomeranians to the park after a rough day at the office, fate steps in. An unlikely hero comes to the rescue when one of her dogs gets loose. Short, pale, and kind of cute, Seth doesn't have a lot of confidence with the ladies, but he hits it off with Patrice. But some things might be too good to be true. While Patrice wonders if Seth could possibly be "the one", fate steps in again with a horrible twist. Will it be a deal breaker or just a storm before bright blue skies?

"Fresh and charming - a heart-warming must read romance." - Sandy Barker, author of *A Sunrise Over Bali*.

"Scotsman in the Stacks is a delightfully sweet, cosy romance for book lovers." - Kiley Dunbar, author of *The Borrow a Bookshop Holiday*

For fans of low-angst, slow burn, closed door romance.

Paige wants two things: to land a full time librarian job and find the man of her dreams. On the cusp of thirty, she finds herself suddenly single and working part-time in a Michigan library. A handsome patron with a delicious accent appears at the reference desk, inadvertently sparking an idea that might help her land the promotion she so desperately needs. But that's not the only thing he sparks.

James is in town from Glasgow, Scotland, on a summer artist residency. Luckily, the trip got him away from the pressure he feels to take over his uncle's river tour business. He only wanted to clear his head and make his art in peace, but he wasn't counting on finding an attractive librarian to fill his days.

With only eight weeks before James goes home to Scotland, Paige knows she should protect her heart. After all, she already wasted years with her commitment-phobe ex. But the more she gets to know James, the less she can stick to her plan to just be friends. Is she just wasting her time again, or can they bridge the ocean between them to find a happily ever after of their own?

"I loved this book - and by 'loved,' I mean I devoured Scotsman in the Stacks in a matter of hours." - *NetGalley Reviewer*

"A very cute, feel-good book with Hallmark movie energy." *-NetGalley Reviewer*

"This is a sweet, uplifting romantic comedy that is perfect if you want something light and fun." - *NetGalley Reviewer*

The Interview
ALANA OXFORD

A job interview has the potential to be life changing, but can it also lead to a happy ever after?

Charlotte just knows she's nailed the job interview for her dream job. She can practically taste it as she walks back to her car. An unexpected series of unlucky events leaves Charlotte doubting everything, but is all hope lost, or is she about to be served a twist she could never imagine?